ERICA ORLOFF

is the author of *Spanish Disco, Diary of a Blues Goddess* and *Divas Don't Fake It (and Nine Other Things I Learned Before I Turned Thirty)*, all published by Red Dress Ink. She is also the author of the gangland novel *The Roofer*, published by MIRA Books, and the vampire novel *Urban Legend* (Silhouette Bombshell). Like the character of Teddi, Erica knows how to score boxing on the ten-point must system, and she is an avid card player. She lives in Florida in a completely chaotic household of family and unruly pets, and she can be reached at www.ericaorloff.com.

mafia chic

Erica Orloff

RED DRESS INK™

First edition September 2004

MAFIA CHIC

A Red Dress Ink novel

ISBN 0-373-25070-3

www.RedDressInk.com

Printed in U.S.A.

Dedicated to my own special kind of family.
And to Pamela Morrell, honorary family member.

ACKNOWLEDGMENTS

As always, a huge thank-you to my agent, Jay Poynor. He has always been my biggest supporter.

Thanks also to Margaret Marbury, for her absolutely brilliant eye, and to Jessica Regante at Red Dress Ink. A note of thanks to Laura Morris, marketing genius at Red Dress Ink, who appreciated the heroine of this tale. Thanks to Dianne Moggy (we still have to go out for spaghetti and meatballs), part of the great network of support I have for my books, as well as publisher Donna Hayes, for her vision. I also have to say this cover is my favorite of all my books so far—so a special thank-you to the terrific designers at Harlequin in Toronto.

You can't write a novel about a special kind of family without having a tight-knit one of your own. Thank you to my parents, Maryanne and Walter Orloff, Stacey, Jessica, extended family members, Gloria and Joey, and the memories of my grandparents, Robert and Irene Cunningham. Wherever my grandmother is, along with my grandfather, they're likely playing pinochle. Love to all my nieces and nephews: Tyler, Zachary, Pannos, Cassidy, Tori.

To the members of Writer's Cramp, Pam Morrell, Gina De Luca, Jon Van Zile, thank you for faithfully meeting every two weeks. I know the food and wine are enticements, but it's also the hard work we do. Your comments are always dead-on.

My friends, Cleo, Nancy, Mark DiBona (my resident bookie and gambling expert), Kathy Levinson, Kathy Johnson and Chris Richardson, for being rock-solid supports.

And last but not least, Alexa, Nicholas and Isabella, for being truly happy and extraordinary little people. And to J.D. For it all.

Preface

Every other Friday from the time I was born until I was sixteen and allowed to start dating, I slept over at my grandma and Poppy Marcello's house. My brother slept over, too, and my parents used the free night to go out for dinner and have some time alone.

My brother and Poppy used to go down to my grandfather's wood shop and make birdhouses. Then they'd watch the fights on cable or would play checkers. My grandmother and I cooked in anticipation for Sunday's big family meal, hand rolling meatballs with chopped veal and beef and bread crumbs. She taught me all the secret family recipes, passed down from her mother and her mother before that.

After cooking, Grandma and I would go sit in the den and have sweetened iced tea in summer or hot tea with lots of milk in winter. One Friday night, when I was about eleven, I remember dragging out the heavy family photo albums lining the bookshelves. I brought one over to her on the couch and plopped next to her and opened it.

"What's this a picture of?" I asked on the first page.

"Oh…" Her eyes misted over, and her smile was bittersweet. "My goodness, but the time flies, Teddi. That was your mother's fifth birthday party. Your grandfather… Every birthday had to be better than the last one. That was the year we had pony rides."

"Wow." I wanted a pony. I turned the pages, and each photo brought on a story. I knew most of the tales already, but I never got tired of curling up next to my grandmother and hearing them again. Then I found a page that had somehow gotten stuck to the page before it. Gingerly, I pried the pages apart. There, in black-and-white photos, was a man I had never seen before. "Who's that?" I asked.

Grandma's eyes welled up, and she heaved an uncharacteristic sigh. "That, my darling, is my youngest brother. He's your great-uncle Mario."

"And who's that lady next to him? She's beautiful."

"Yes, she is. Was. That woman is Mariella."

"How come I don't know them? How come I've never met your brother, Grandma?"

"He was struck by the thunderbolt."

I looked up at my grandmother's face, still relatively unlined, rosy-cheeked, her dark hair, graying at the temples, pulled up in a topknot and secured with bobby pins. I furrowed my brow. "A thunderbolt? He was hit by lightning?"

She laughed, even as she dabbed her eyes with a little handkerchief she kept in her apron pocket. "No…it's an expression we Italians have. When you're older, you'll fall in love and get married. Maybe it will be someone you've known a long time…a friend you suddenly see in a different light. Or maybe you'll go off to college and meet a boy you could imagine yourself spending the rest of your life with. Someone with good values. But maybe…just maybe…you will be struck by the thunderbolt. That means you'll look across a crowded room, or you'll bump into someone on the street…and from the very second you look into his eyes and he looks into yours, that's it. You know. *He* is the one. It won't make any sense. People will tell you that you're crazy, but you will know. There'll be this voice, this feeling deep inside…you will just know, and your life will never be the same, because none of it will matter until you finally get to be with him. Your love."

I looked down at the picture of my long-lost uncle Mario. "So what happened to him?"

"He's in prison, dear."

"Prison? For what?"

She hesitated, and then said, "He killed a man." She said it as if she'd said, "He ran a red light."

I shivered slightly and snuggled closer to her. "Why? How?"

"Oh…it's a long story." She looked at me, and I clearly wasn't going to let the matter drop. "All right, then. Your uncle Mario saw Mariella at a dance. And that was it. They were both struck by the thunderbolt. You've never seen two people more in love than your uncle Mario and Mariella. It was like electricity ran between them. When people were around them, it was intoxicating. You could just *feel* the way they were meant to be together."

I hung on her every word. "And?"

"Mariella's father was not a reasonable man. A very over-protective Sicilian. But a little crazy, too. He decided Uncle Mario was not the man he wanted Mariella to marry. He had already decided she should marry Joey Antonelli."

"The plumber?" Everyone in our neighborhood knew Antonelli and Sons plumbing. Their vans—all a bright yellow—were always on the streets of Brooklyn.

"Yes. The plumber. Anyway, Mariella's father sent her two older brothers to scare Uncle Mario. They went to beat him up."

"Oh, no!"

"Yes." She nodded. "Only they didn't count on Uncle Mario being so strong and so in love. It was like he was superhuman. He turned around and beat one of her brothers so hard he killed him right there on the street."

I shuddered. "But…but couldn't he tell the police it was only because they were going to beat him up?"

"Yes. He did say it was self-defense. But…the beating was so brutal. And Uncle Mario didn't have a mark on him. And it was around the time that…well…the judge wanted to teach a lesson to our kind."

"Our kind?"

"The family. It's too much for you to understand. But it didn't go well, the trial. They added some other charges—racketeering. Anyway, he got a prison sentence."

"And he's still in jail?"

"Yes. He's eligible for parole next year."

"And what about Mariella? Did she marry Joey Antonelli like her father wanted?"

Grandma shook her head.

"Well, what happened to her?"

"She stood by Uncle Mario. She had no choice. She'd been struck by the thunderbolt. She was very sad about her brother, but she still loved Uncle Mario. Her family disowned her. She ended up moving away. She visits Uncle Mario every weekend. She dresses all in black. People say she's crazy. She dresses like a widow. She missed any opportunity to marry like her friends, to have babies. Waiting…waiting…all this time. Like a penance or something."

"But they'll get to be together when he comes out of prison. They'll finally be together."

"Yes. But…well, they'll never be those two young people so in love." Suddenly, Grandma seemed to think better of telling me the story of Uncle Mario and Mariella. "Oh…what am I telling you this sad story for?" She patted my knee. "It's in your blood, you know. The passion. Maybe you'll be struck by the thunderbolt yourself. Maybe you will have that kind of love."

I looked down at the picture of my uncle Mario and the beautiful, tragic Mariella. And I knew one thing. I never, *ever* wanted to be struck by the thunderbolt.

chapter 1

"Jackson is going to take a dive in round three," I said, glancing at the television as I passed through the living room, where my roommate sat with her boyfriend of the moment, a boxing buff.

Dave eyed me the way men do when they assume a woman doesn't know the first thing about sports or the difference between a Phillips head and flat-head screwdriver (for the record, the Phillips head is shaped like a cross on the end). "Jackson? A lot you know about boxing. He'll go all twelve and take the decision."

I stopped in my tracks and whirled around. "Wanna bet?"

"I hate to rob you of your hard-earned money, Teddi, but you're on. Five bucks says he'll go the distance."

"Then let's make it interesting. Hundred bucks...*and* the loser cleans the kitchen." I stood in the doorway of the living room and cast a backward glance to the kitchen, where a porcelain tower of dishes was precariously leaning in the sink.

"A hundred bucks?" He was handsome, I'd give Diana that. Nice biceps. But then Diana always had handsome men following her around. I called her Lady Di, and her British accent, Paris fashions and catlike eyes made her stand out, even among New York City's trendsetters. However, something about this guy annoyed me. He was too cocky, a trait I was certain Lady Di would discover very quickly. She tolerates fools and assholes less than I do.

"Yes. A hundred bucks *and* the dishes. Unless you're afraid a *woman* will beat you," I said, emphasizing "woman" as if I had said "herpes" or "vomit."

"You're on."

I strode across the living room and stuck out my hand. "Then shake on it."

Dave shook, firmly I might add, and I sat down on the love seat to watch the boxing match. "What round is it?" I asked.

"Second." Lady Di spoke up, her smirk barely contained. She knew that, other faults aside, I never took a sucker bet.

The bell signaled the end of round two. Jackson looked to be in terrific shape. His muscular back and coffee-colored skin glistened with sweat, but he wasn't even breathing heavy. His opponent, "Rocky" Garcia, was nine years older—a lifetime in boxing years, sort of like dog years—and he already looked tired. The guy was known as a "bleeder," sustaining cuts above the eye that would pour down his face, blocking his vision. If you've never actually watched a boxing match, then you might not know cuts like that entail sticking a Q-tip directly *into* the gash. Boxing is not for the squeamish. And though Garcia was the champ, no one expected him to win against Jackson.

Dave leaned back on the couch and stretched. "I'm going to take Diana out to Whiskey Blue with our hundred bucks—which we'll blow on a bottle of champagne. And we'll tell you *all* about it in the morning."

I rolled my eyes, then focused on the television set. When the bell rang, Garcia came out with a flurry. Left, right, left jab. Uppercut. The announcers were getting excited, shouting into their microphones. The crowd in the MGM Grand in Vegas rose to their collective feet. Jackson shook his head from side to side, as if to clear it from the small pounding he took. Garcia came at him again with a series of body blows and then—wham!—Jackson hit the canvas like a man who'd just had a safe fall on him in a cartoon. He was caught square on the jaw.

Dave leaned forward on the couch, in shock, screaming at the television set. He stood up and leaned still closer to the TV, not believing his eyes. "Get up, you loser! Get up!" Dave was willing the fighter to climb the ropes and stand again, in the way men have of believing the athletes on television can actually *hear* them through some miracle of technology. But Jackson just lay there, as I knew he would. The fight was called, the champ held up the belt he retained with the victory, and I stuck out my palm.

"A cool one hundred, please."

Stunned, Dave pulled his eel-skin wallet out of the back pocket of his beautifully cut pants (Italian, no doubt). Lady Di tried to look appropriately sad that he lost, but she couldn't look at me for fear we would both dissolve into gales of laughter.

"Here," Dave said through his teeth, seething. He handed me five twenties.

"Fastest hundred I ever earned. Thanks…and Dave?"

"What," he said evenly.

"Don't forget the kitchen," I replied in a singsong voice. "You'll find everything you need under the sink…sponges, dish towels and detergent." I twirled around and veritably pranced into my bedroom and shut the door. I looked at my clock radio—10:37 p.m. I gave Dave ten minutes before he left and slammed the door.

He only took five.

Lady Di knocked on my bedroom door a moment later and poked her head in. "What an insufferable ass," she said, then squealed with laughter and flopped down on my bed.

"He deserved it."

She squeezed my hand. "You are something else, Teddi ol' girl. This calls for champagne cocktails."

She climbed off my bed, went into the still-dirty kitchen and returned with two champagne flutes with sugar cubes nestled in the bottom, a splash of bitters on each and a bottle of Moët. She popped the cork and poured us each a glass right to the rim.

"To Teddi, for knowing much more about boxing than Dave will ever know—and to her hundred dollars."

"And to my grandfather Marcello, for owning Tony 'the Dancer' Jackson—and to Garcia."

We clinked glasses and sipped the bubbly champagne. Lady Di sat down on the antique rocking chair in the corner of my room, next to a small pie table I inherited from my great-grandmother and covered in pictures of family and friends encased in silver frames.

"You're always complaining about your family, Teddi, but it seems to me they come in terribly handy at times. My parents are pathetically boring—so utterly devoid of any life. Their faces are so stiff, they look like Botox patients whose treatment went horribly awry. I'd much rather be in your family. The food on Sundays is better, too."

"Well…you're an honorary member, anyway. They adore you. But trust me, you really wouldn't want to be in my family if you had a choice. My childhood wasn't about snooty British boarding schools, Miss Fancy Pants. I didn't learn to ride English on Thoroughbred horses, and I didn't ski in St. Moritz on vacation."

In fact, Di knew very well that I learned three-card monte before I started kindergarten. I learned how to score a boxing match on the ten-point must system before I learned my ABCs—and it wasn't too long after that when I found out most of the matches were fixed. I know about the over-under in football, and I can shoot pool better than Minnesota Fats—well, maybe not him, but I can outshoot almost anyone. This does not make for a) an idyllic childhood or b) the kind of skills you like to show off to men. I mean, on what date do you tell the man you potentially want to sleep with that before you discuss birth control it might be a good idea to see how he feels about the Witness Protection Program?

"Hmm." Lady Di frowned, squinting her blue, almost-violet eyes. "I'd hate to give up my ski vacations. Nonetheless, your family is much more fun than my own pathetic 'rents."

"Maybe, but then there's the little problem of surveillance. Go to the window."

"Oh, not again." She shook her head. "Don't tell me…"

"Go on. Peek out the blinds."

She did as I asked.

"Let me guess, Di. A long, black Lincoln Town Car? A guy leaning on the hood? He's sort of just hanging around—maybe even reading a newspaper?"

"You know very well that, yes, he's there. Appears to be your cousin Anthony—who I will reiterate for the thousandth time is very hunky, by the way—and your uncle Lou again."

"Of course, because we two nice single girls shouldn't be living alone in the big city."

"Puts a crimp in things, doesn't it?"

"Tell me about it."

"You'd think they would have grown tired of this by now."

"Please…my uncle Tony once waited fifteen years to extract revenge from a guy who screwed him in a casino deal in Atlantic City. My family is nothing if not patient."

Lady Di and I had moved in together two years ago when my father "persuaded" someone to rent us this place for a song. I realize how extremely hypocritical it is to complain about my family at the same time that I enjoy a two-bedroom apartment with a view of the East River in a doorman building. Of course, the spacious apartment and the view came with the vigilant watchdog eyes of various members of my family. My cousin Tony—whom Di has a crush on, and vice versa—seemed to have drawn the short straw or something as he is the one who watches over us the most.

Lady Di came over to the bed and sat down. "So we ignore them. There's nothing exciting going on here, anyway. Eventually, they'll go home. What do you say we hit some clubs tomorrow, Teddi? It's your night off."

"I don't know."

"Please," she pleaded, "I have a smashing new outfit that I'm dying to wear. And now that Dave appears to be out of the picture, you can't expect me to spend the brisk and bitter days of autumn in New York alone, can you? It'll be winter before you know it."

"No, I suppose I can't. Though Lord knows I'll be by my lonesome."

"Don't say that, Teddi." She smiled and refilled my glass. Standing up, she kissed me on the top of my head. "I have a feeling you'll meet the right one before long. See you in the morning, love."

"Good night, Lady Di."

She shut my bedroom door. I turned on my stereo and listened to a vintage Bruce Springsteen CD. I stripped and pulled on a sleep shirt, then I padded over to the window. Tony was pacing the sidewalk. I knew he and my uncle would stay another hour, then head over to Mario's for some pizza and a card game.

I went into my bathroom—*my* bathroom…in New York City where most people live in apartments the *size* of bathrooms. Our apartment has floor-to-ceiling windows, crown molding, Ralph Lauren paint and hardwood floors glossed to a sheen. I washed up and brushed my teeth.

Back in my room, I sat on my bed and pulled out a photo album I kept on the shelf near my bed. In my life, I hit the crime-family genetic lottery. My mother's family, the Marcellos, own one of the largest pizza chains in New York. They also are bookies and gamblers, loan sharks and pool hustlers. Suspected of money laundering, they are what New York newspapers call "an alleged crime family."

Flipping through the album, I thought back on the birthday parties in the pictures I had slid into plastic photo sheets. Other little girls had parties with ponies and pizza, clowns and confetti. I had parties that lasted until the morning of the day after. I had ponies, too, and cake with real whipped cream frosting, and spumoni. But there was always a craps game going on in the basement, or even the occasional fist-fight between the Marcellos and the Gallos.

Turning another page in the album, I landed on photos of my cousin Marie Gallo's wedding. The Gallo clan was Sicilian—which some might think is the same as Italian, but it's not—at least not in Brooklyn. Where the Marcellos were prone to angry outbursts, the Gallos were always picking on one another and pulling elaborate practical jokes, all in good fun—until the fistfights started, usually for reasons no one could remember the morning after. Two of my father's six brothers were on the fringes of the five families. My uncle Jackie and uncle Tommy are both serving hard time in prison for murder. My father managed to squeak through life with a rap sheet a mile long but no major convictions. I can't say what he actually does for a living. Not because I won't say, but rather I *can't* say, as in I'm not quite sure. How-ever, because of the family, I grew up hearing clicks on the telephone because we were bugged, and catching sight of unmarked federal cars in my rearview mirror as I learned to drive.

I sipped my champagne and crinkled up my face. Cham-pagne and Crest toothpaste don't mix. I swallowed another swig anyway and sighed. In between these two crazy fam-ilies was me, a mix of both. I had inherited dark masses of curly Italian hair from the Marcellos and the olive skin of the Gallos. Green-eyed (a Sicilian trait), I have a very ethnic look—whatever that means. I've been told, by less-than-gra-cious dates—and haven't I had enough of those?—that I look like I "just got off the boat." And when I get fed up with said lousy dates, when I want to see whether or not a man is *really* interested in me, I say that on my mother's side, I am one of *the* Marcellos. That usually makes most men turn pale.

Because while all this may sound delightfully colorful, it ceased to be even remotely amusing when I became an adolescent. Suddenly, I had to explain my "family," in more ways than one. And bringing a date home to meet the Gallos or the Marcellos was like subjecting the poor, hapless guy to an FBI interrogation. My male relatives would corner my date to find out his intentions. My solution? Stop dating. (Not really.) I just became as devious as my family—only far less criminal. I hid my dating from everyone. Lady Di became my conspirator from the moment we met when we were freshmen in college. Once we moved to this apartment, I also relied on my doorman, Michel, to frequently slip me out the back of my apartment building, enticing him with fresh cannolis from his favorite bakery.

I shut the photo album. Walking over to the window, I saw that my cousin Tony and uncle Lou had left for the night. They had my best interests at heart. They all did. But both sides of the family were pressuring me to marry and have babies. And while I did feel a baby urge when I saw mothers and their rosy-cheeked little cherubs in Central Park, the likelihood of ever meeting anyone who would find my extraordinary three-card monte skills endearing—let alone maternal—was not likely. And what man in his right mind is going to sleep with a woman whose father says, "You hurt her, we'll break your legs"—and means it? The truth is that despite America's obsession with all things Mafia, from the *Godfather* to the *Sopranos,* being a Mafia princess is most decidedly not what it is cracked up to be.

chapter 2

"So I hear a man was over at your apartment last night."

It was my mother, of course, calling me at work to remind me that my biological clock was tick, tick-tocking away.

"Gee, wonder where you'd hear that from?"

"A little bird told me."

"Little? Uncle Lou weighs a good 250 pounds, Ma."

"Does it matter where I heard it from? Just tell me who he was."

"Mother, how many times must I tell you I'm a lesbian?"

She audibly sighed at my feeble attempt to throw her off my trail. My mother feels the need to call me once a day, whether we have anything to say to each other or not—and we usually don't.

"Don't give me that crap, young lady."

"Ma…I have a million things to do." Out of the corner of my eye, I could see the morning vegetables being delivered. My cousin Quinn and I own "Teddi's," a little Italian bistro just barely in the black. We're struggling to survive in a city with restaurants on every corner and sky-high rents. The fact we rent from family does help things a bit. I cook. Quinn runs the front of the house and tries to bang all the waitresses. He's good at both.

"'A million things to do…a million things to do.' But apparently one of them is not to tell her mother about the man in her apartment last night."

"He was Lady Di's date, Ma."

"Oh." Her voice was flat, emotionless—and spoke volumes. My older brother Michael moved out to Hollywood to become an actor. He lucked into a couple of minor roles and has a recurring bit as the boyfriend of a character on a WB television show. He never visits home, and we spot him in cheesy tabloid magazines squiring beautiful but vapid actresses around town. His idea of commitment is staying for breakfast, and, assuming he knows what a condom is, there's not a chance that he's going to settle down and make my parents happy by marrying and having a baby. Which leaves, reluctantly, me.

"You don't have to sound like that, Ma. The guy was a jerk, anyway."

"Jerk, schmerk," she said. "You can reform a jerk. Look what I did with your father. You need to stop being so picky, Theresa Marie."

Ah, the dreaded official first name and—worse—the use of my middle name. This was serious—at least where my mother was concerned.

"Ma…I will find someone eventually, but I'm not in any hurry." Sure, let me get struck by the thunderbolt and end up visiting prison in widow's garb. Not a chance. "Besides, Ma, running this place takes up so much of my time. I barely have enough time to sleep. I eat standing up.... I'm not looking for a relationship."

"Theresa...darling—" My mother continued nagging. "You're not getting any younger—and neither am I! I want grandbabies. I want to see my daughter walk down the aisle. Is this so wrong, Theresa? Isn't this what every mother dreams of? I just want you to be as happy as your father and I are. I want you to have someone to grow old with."

I tried to avoid howling into the phone with laughter. My mother and father can't be in the same room without arguing. She henpecks at him constantly, and he hollers that he can't enjoy any peace in his own home. He hates the plastic slipcovers on our furniture, and she hates the fact that he'll drop a thousand on the ponies. They sleep in twin beds. Have for as long as I can remember. Not exactly a ringing endorsement for the institution of marriage. I am convinced Michael and I are, for the record, immaculate conceptions. Something in the water in Brooklyn.

"I'll get a cat."

"Not funny, Theresa Marie. Not funny at all. Do you like to torture your own mother like this? To break my heart in every phone call?"

When my mother talks, I envision the old *Peanuts* specials whenever the teacher spoke. "Mwah, mwah-mwah, mwah-mwah." I tuned her out.

"No, Ma, I don't. Listen, it's getting busy here. Let me go."

"I wish you never got into the restaurant business. It's not right for a woman."

"Please, Ma...I was born with it in my blood."

"You coming Sunday?"

"If I didn't, there'd be a hit ordered. Of course I'm coming." Sunday was an eating extravaganza that most Americans reserve for an occasion like Thanksgiving. The piles of food are downright nauseating. Attendance was pretty close to mandatory.

"And how many places should I set?" she asked hopefully.

"Two. One for me…and one for Lady Di."

"Even if it's short notice, if you meet someone, there's always room for another plate at the table."

"I know, Ma. Thanks. Gotta run."

I replaced the receiver on the hook. She never gave up. She married at eighteen, right after high school. I don't know if she was struck by the thunderbolt. Hard to picture someone feeling that way for my father with his ugly bowling shirts and beer belly. Still, to my mother, her husband and family are everything to her. When Michael and I were little, we were her universe. But if she only saw what I saw. The health spa where I take the occasional yoga class in an attempt to convince myself I'm not getting out of shape is a perfect example. A microcosm of pickup lines and outright seduction. A revolving door of hookups. Everyone has baggage. Failed marriages and relationships, messed-up childhoods, resentments and unhappiness. But I lug around a *steamer trunk* of baggage. I'm from a family of "made" men and wise guys, with a true nut job or two thrown in for good measure. Do you bring this up with a date over dinner? Dessert? When it starts to get serious? And even if a man *thinks* he can handle my background, he's just kidding himself. Spending time with my father makes all those movie mobsters look like pussycats. He *frightens* people.

The phone rang again. It was Lady Di.

"Hello Teddi, ol' girl," she said, as if we were going to meet for a fox hunt.

"Hey…what's going on?"

"I am bored out of my mind." Lady Di works as a PR agent, which means she has invitations to all of New York's hot spots. But as much as she likes the night life, she loathes being in the office. I accuse her of being part vampire. She abhors daylight.

"Sorry. I just got off the phone with my mother, who reminded me yet again that I am depriving her of the chance to see me in virginal white gracefully gliding down the aisle and into a happy life like her and my father. I could hear my ovaries shriveling as we talked."

"She never gives up, does she? My parents are too afraid to say anything like that to me. It's decidedly un-British. Sticking their noses in like that. Besides, if they make me angry, I'll never visit them again. As it is I hate that damn drafty house and the sons of their equally stiff friends. Besides, the thought of marriage and babies gives me hives."

"Well, my parents have never kept their opinions to themselves."

"All right, ol' girl. I've got just the ticket for your ennui. We're going to Shangri-la tonight."

"What?" Shangri-la was the hottest bar of the moment, in a city where "the moment" changes faster than the revolving door at Macy's.

"Yes, my little Mafia darling! Lady Di has done it again. So what will you wear?"

I sighed. Lady Di tried to dress me in fuck-me pumps, a micromini and a halter top with a "jaunty" scarf tied around my neck…some sort of Euro-look, with bright red lipstick and sultry, smoky eyes to boot. However, she just could not transform me into a mystery woman. She could carry off a look like she was born on Page Six of the *Post,* where she actually appears from time to time. Me? Between my unruly hair and my slightly lopsided smile, my dimples (which admittedly are cute—but cute isn't what we're aiming for) and full cheeks, I always look like I'm playing dress-up.

"I don't know, Di. I'll figure it out when I get home."

"Think about it, darling. Because I have a feeling tonight will be lucky. My Chinese horoscope says so."

Leave it to Lady Di. The regular zodiac doesn't do. She consults the Chinese version. She's a dragon. I'm a mouse or a rodent of some sort. Need I say more?

"Well, let me go, Di. I need to start today's soup."

"Kisses, love!"

"Back at you."

Much as I adored her—with all my heart—she just didn't understand. She only heard from her parents once a month, if that. They saw one another every other year. Remembering my conversation with my mother, I rolled my eyes. Lady Di had no idea just how lucky she was.

Shangri-la was packed with the black-clad denizens of Manhattan. The women all seemed to be tall (I'm only five foot four) and anorexic, and the men looked like refugees from the fashion spreads in *GQ*. But Lady Di, of course, had access to the VIP room, where we promptly headed. She spotted one of the owners, a restaurant impresario who always filled his restaurants and clubs with supermodels, hip-hop stars and A-list Hollywood. He immediately gave us a table and sent over a bottle of champagne. Lady Di's PR skills were unparalleled. She knew all the right people, and she charmed the ones she didn't know until they couldn't resist her. And unlike a few other "über-bitches" who worked PR in New York City, she somehow managed to do it by being tough yet never alienating anyone. It also didn't hurt that her father was wealthy beyond imagination—even if, as she put it—he was as "stiff as a piece of plywood."

We sat down, and our champagne was uncorked and placed in an ice bucket. Lady Di was dressed in a simple black minidress with a Hermès scarf wrapped around her thick blond hair. Her makeup wasn't even a brand you could buy in the States. Her father flew to Japan on business regularly; she gave him a list and he bought it there, then shipped it to her. She wasn't someone who dressed outlandishly in the hopes of being the center of attention, yet she had her own distinct style—not to mention perfect porcelain skin. If we weren't best friends, I could hate her.

I had decided, with Lady Di's prodding, to wear a black miniskirt and a silk kimono-style jacket her father brought me back from Japan on Lady Di's orders. It was a brilliant blue, and though I felt out of place in New York with its sea of black clothes, it did feel beautiful on, and I caught admiring glances. I envisioned myself, for a change, as glamorous, rather than like the Italian girl from Brooklyn with the mass of unruly hair. I had even blown dry my hair nice and straight, and it had cooperated for once.

We sipped champagne, and Di leaned in close to me and gave a running commentary on every person who walked past.

"A-list actor… Cocaine fiend."

"That one's wife left him for another woman."

As for the women: "Fake tits…real…real…oh, my God, fake. They're like boulders perched there."

She went on: "Does she not own a mirror? She'll be in

the next edition of *Us Weekly* under the 'what was she thinking?' category."

"Her hairdresser should be shot."

All right, taken out of context, she sounded catty, but she just likes to "dish." I bet she could make even the guards at Buckingham Palace laugh, if given the chance.

Suddenly a WASPish blonde approached our table. "Robert Wharton." He smiled. "And you two appear to be the only interesting women in this place. Can I join you?" We were seated on a bloodred velvet couch, and Di immediately scrunched closer to me.

"Okay…we've moved on over. But you can only join us if you are terribly amusing and promise to make us laugh," Di said, and smiled.

"Promise."

Turned out Robert Wharton, who looked vaguely familiar, was an on-air reporter for a major cable news network. He had the bland yet handsome looks of a news anchor, a side part in his perfect hair, and an angular build encased in an expensive suit jacket. His chin was dimpled, and his nose was straight without a trace of ethnicity. Everyone in my family looked like they had been on the wrong end of a strong right hook. His hazel eyes peered out from behind wire-rimmed glasses.

"I scored the first post-trial interview with Connie Benson," he said when Di pressed him to tell us just where we'd seen him before.

"Oh, my God! The Hamptons Harlot!"

Connie Benson was a 40DD porno actress who married the king of Long Island real estate, who promptly died under questionable circumstances. And despite a murder trial that lasted for six months and riveted the media, she'd been acquitted, though the prosecutors had thought it was a no-brainer.

"So dish. Do you think she did it?" Di asked.

He nodded.

"Well…" I chimed in, "she's laughing all the way to the bank. He froze out his kids in the will."

Robert nodded. "And she has the spending habits of a Rockefeller. She went through a cool half million just adding mirrored ceilings in all the bedrooms, and her own state-of-the-art screening room. She likes to watch her old porn movies with popcorn and her new lover. The old man was forty years older than she. This new guy is only nineteen."

"Truth is always stranger than fiction," I said.

"I'm so glad you sat down," Di added. "I was hooked on that case. Watched the recaps every night on Court TV. Cheers!" She lifted her glass and elbowed me to lift mine, and the three of us toasted.

"You look familiar, too." Robert studied me.

I wriggled uncomfortably in my seat. Of course, he could have eaten in my restaurant and have recognized me out of context. But A&E also profiled my family a year ago, complete with family trees and fuzzy photos. Because I was the only granddaughter of Angelo Marcello in a sea of seventeen male cousins, I had been filmed from a distance crossing the street and labeled "The Mafia Princess."

"Do you work out at Parallel Spa?"

He shook his head. We were all growing hoarse talking over the music.

"Ever eat at a tiny little place called Teddi's?"

"No. Where is it?"

"East Side. Mid-Sixties."

He shook his head. "You work there?"

Lady Di wrapped an arm around me. "She *owns* it. And it has absolutely the most delicious food in New York City. I would starve without Teddi. Would curl up on the floor and die. Her spaghetti carbonara is rapturous."

I rolled my eyes. "Spoken like a true PR agent."

Robert laughed. "Well, sounds like I should visit Teddi's, but...I still feel like I know you from somewhere."

"No, I don't think we've met before," I said firmly.

"But now we have. Can I invite you to dinner? I promise I'm not a serial killer. Just an honest boy from Philadelphia."

Di dug her heel into my instep, urging me to say yes. I glared at her, then nodded at Robert.

We spent the rest of the night making small talk. Turned out the "honest boy" from Philadelphia was from Main Line Philly and old money. I cringed. Talk about worlds colliding. We ordered more champagne and discovered that Robert liked horses, specifically polo, and had attended the University of Pennsylvania's Wharton Business School. And yes, there was some relation to the original Wharton way back in his lineage.

"Is Teddi your real name?" he shouted over the music.

I shook my head. "Theresa. But my grandfather called me Teddi Bear, ridiculous as that sounds, and it stuck." Of course, I didn't point out that Angelo Marcello, one of the most celebrated of the old-time mobsters, was my Poppy. I was his teddy bear, his angel, and if anyone thought about touching a hair on my head, there wouldn't be a federal safe house safe enough for the man, whoever he was.

"That's really cute."

I shrugged. "I like it better than Theresa, that's for sure."

Lady Di stood and waved to a client. "Back in a jiff, Teddi."

Robert focused on me again. "I wish I could place you. I just have this feeling we've met before."

"I promise you, we haven't."

"I know this is the oldest line in the book, Teddi, but if we haven't met before, then I have a serious case of déjà vu. I must have known you in another life."

He was near enough to me that when he bent his head to better hear me, I could smell his cologne. Maybe it was the loud music, but he leaned in so close to me that he gave the impression that he wanted to hear every word I said.

"Maybe…" Anxious to change the subject, to steer him away from the Marcello and Gallo family names, I asked him how he got into journalism.

"Please. Every kid who ever saw *All the President's Men* wanted to be the next Woodward or Bernstein and packed off to college…and I was no exception. I changed my major from business. I found I had the stomach for journalism. I wasn't squeamish at crime scenes. I didn't mind working my way up from the bottom. I was always comfortable at public speaking, so speaking in front of a camera wasn't a big deal."

"I'd rather do just about anything than speak in front of a group of people."

"Number-one fear for most people."

Should I tell him that in my neighborhood, the number-one fear is having my uncle Lou show up to collect a bad debt? I opted to shut up.

Around two o'clock in the morning, I realized my alarm was going to ring mighty early for opening the restaurant. By this time, Di had rejoined us, and we'd ordered another bottle of champagne. As we poured the last of it into our glasses, I nudged Di and said we had better go.

"What time is it?" Robert pushed up the cuff of his shirt and read his Rolex. "Jesus! The night flew by."

We all stood. Robert kissed my cheek, took a card from the restaurant and promised to call to arrange dinner. (If I had a dollar for every time I've heard that line, I could have bailed out my uncle Jackie the last time he was arraigned.)

Lady Di and I said goodbye and made our way through the packed main club, its dance floor so crowded you couldn't fit a slip of paper between the dancers, and went outside. The doorman hailed us a cab. Nestled into the back, Di was both drunk and ecstatic for me.

"Robert Wharton…old money, handsome and a high-profile job on top of it. I think this is your lucky night, Teddi, you Chinese mouse, you! Or is it a rat?"

"Lady Di," I slurred, the champagne long since gone to my head. I could only imagine the hell of standing over a hot stove the next day. "Given the unfortunate incarceration of half my family, and the fact that there are one hundred hijacked Betsey Johnson dresses in the basement of my parents' house, do you really think a high-profile relationship is such a good idea?"

"Fuck it all," she said. "Then a toss in the hay and you're done with him. But really, Teddi, do they expect you to marry a mobster?"

I frowned. "No…I guess not."

"Trust me, darling. He seemed positively mad about you. If this works out, your parents will be delighted."

"I doubt it. But let's take it one step at a time."

As the cabbie raced through the streets of Manhattan, I tried to quell the feelings of nausea in my stomach. But whether it was from the champagne or the prospect of telling "old money" Robert Wharton about my family tree, I wasn't exactly sure.

The next day I walked the twenty blocks to work. I'm one of the few New Yorkers blessed with an easy commute—a brisk walk instead of clinging to a subway strap for dear life, or exhaust fumes filling my nostrils as I ride the bus. The only tough thing is three days a week I work early. As in really early.

At six-thirty, on three hours' sleep, and my head pounding as if some heavy-metal drummer had taken up residence in my left temple, I was already starting a pot of gravy—what we Italians call spaghetti sauce—which would be used for the manicotti, as well as several pasta dishes. I took out fresh parsley and began chopping, finding a rhythm as the sharp knife hit the cutting board—chop, chop, chop—my fingers curled to control the blade. My cousin Quinn only worked nights, and the sous chef, Leon, wasn't due in until nine-thirty, so I had the place to myself. Leon favored a serious hip-hop station on the radio. Chopping to DMX and Eminem can be kind of therapeutic. It can also get on your nerves. So I spent my mornings alone in silence, humming to myself, thinking of nothing in particular. This morning, however, I was thinking that Lady Di and her wild nightlife were going to be the death of me very soon. And I was thinking that Robert Wharton was very cute in a nonethnic kind of way. I couldn't imagine someone with the last name of Wharton being struck by the thunderbolt. Somehow, I found that comforting—if he even called, which I doubted. So I put him from my mind and concentrated on the simmering pot after popping two aspirin.

Next, I busied myself making the soup of the day—a pasta fajioli—then went to the front of the house—restaurant talk for the dining room—and fetched a cold club soda from the bar. I looked around the restaurant—my place. Or at least half mine and half Quinn's. Though to be technical about it, the bank owned a big chunk, too.

I had wanted my own restaurant since I could remember. My grandfather owned a restaurant in Brooklyn, and though he owned it for business reasons—Mafia business reasons—I had spent much of my childhood sitting at its checkered-tablecloth tables, eating authentic food prepared by men who spoke only Italian.

When Quinn and I found our place, it was suffering from neglect. The floors were filthy, the lighting dim and roaches roamed freely across the stainless counters in the kitchen. But Quinn and I saw past all that. Now, with room for twenty-two tables, Teddi's sparkled. We had the walls painted with a faux finish that resembled stone walls, vaguely reminiscent of Florence, sort of ancient-looking. The ivory tablecloths were crisp, and the plates on each table bore handpainted flowers on the rim. When nighttime came and the small votives on each table were lit, with fresh flowers in each bud vase and a crowd at the bar waiting for a table, it was magical. At the end of every shift, Quinn and I would each have a sambuca with three coffee beans floating for good luck and go over the night and unwind. I had never, not even for a moment, wanted to do anything else, despite the long hours. Despite the fact that it was back-breaking sometimes. Despite the fact that I had a hangover and was staring at a double shift.

I went back into the kitchen—my domain—and continued prepping for lunch. Around ten o'clock the back office phone rang. "Teddi's," I answered on line two.

"Is Teddi there? The owner Teddi?"

"Who's calling?" I was used to food and beverage sales guys calling, trying to get our account. Linen companies. Wine sales reps.

"It's Robert Wharton."

"Robert? It's Teddi."

"Thought that was your voice."

I managed to sputter out a hello. A man in Manhattan who actually *called* when he said he would?

"You gave me your card," he offered, as if the reason I sounded a little stunned was I didn't remember him. As if I could forget his anchorman smile.

"Of course." I finally regained my composure. "It's nice to hear from you, Robert."

"Listen…I would love to take you to dinner."

"Um…great." Nit-twit, as Di would call me. So much for witty repartee.

"What's your schedule like?"

"Thursdays are good. I usually work Friday night. My sous chef does Thursday night. I do lunch Thursday instead."

"What about Sunday? I'm off on Sundays."

I crinkled up my face in a wince he couldn't see. Sunday was sacrosanct—family dinner in Brooklyn. "Sundays are no good."

"Thursday then. Next Thursday okay?"

"Sure."

"I'm a little nervous taking a chef out for dinner. You probably have high standards."

"No. I was born in a family of professional eaters. But honestly, I'm not that fussy. I like to enjoy someone else's cooking for a change."

"How about if we meet at a little Japanese place called Yama's at Fifty-fifth and Seventh?"

"I've heard of it." *Heard* of it? I'd heard it was one of the priciest new restaurants in the city—and the sushi chef was a temperamental master. I knew I'd love to scope out their menu. Japanese was a style of cooking I'd longed to experiment with. My mother mocked my Manhattan eating adventures. "Raw fish," she'd once said. "What's next? Cold monkey meat?"

"I'll make reservations for eight-thirty. Okay? Does that sound all right?"

"Okay. See you then."

"I'm really looking forward to it."

"Me, too."

I hung up the phone by pressing down on the reset button. Then I immediately speed-dialed Lady Di on her cell, which she wore attached to her hip at all times, with a tiny little earpiece set in her ear. Di also carried a Palm Pilot and had her laptop at home perpetually plugged in. Besides dressing to the nines, she was wired to the nines.

"Diana Kent here," she answered.

"It's Teddi."

"Hello there, flatmate," she said, never getting used to calling me her roommate or roomie.

"He called."

"Who?"

"Who…*him!*"

"That Robert fellow?"

"Yes, that Robert fellow."

"How fantastic, Teddi! Are you going to see him?"

"Next Thursday."

"Smashing."

"I need your help, though."

"What?" she asked. "Want to borrow my little black dress? Oh…what about the Roberto Cavalli one?"

"Too wild."

"My Donna Karan. The black wraparound one?"

"No. That's not why I called. Well…now that you mention it, that dress might be good. But no…I need you to distract my 'bodyguards.'"

"Right-o. No problem."

"Don't you think it's a little ridiculous that I'm a woman in my mid-twenties and I'm still being baby-sat?"

"Yes. But one of your baby-sitters is your cousin Tony. And I find him positively delicious. So, for purely selfish reasons, I rather find it amusing."

"You're impossible."

"But that's what makes me so irresistible."

"Look, just help me duck out unnoticed."

"You can count on me. I always feel all James Bond when we do this, you know."

"I feel a little Godfatherish when we do it. But either way, next Thursday keep them busy. I'd like to get in a first date without them looking over my shoulder. And the black dress would be nice, too."

"It's yours."

"We have six days to plan."

"And plan we shall. Must run now."

"*Ciao.*" I put the phone down. I had stopped going to church years ago, but if I *was* still a church-goer, I would have said four novenas and five Hail Marys that my date with Robert Wharton went off without a hitch.

chapter 3

Calling what my family does on Sundays "dinner" is like saying the pope is just another priest with a fancier hat.

Lady Di and I arrived at Sunday dinner to the usual chaos of the Marcello clan with a couple of Gallos thrown in for good measure. In the kitchen my mother was making an immense pot of gravy. Not only was the pot big enough for one of my little cousins to use as a fort when not filled with gravy, but Ma couldn't even move it from one burner to the next without the help of my cousin Tony.

My aunt Marie, aunt Gina, aunt Connie and assorted other aunts, and wives and fiancées of my male cousins were all crowded into the kitchen as well, supervising my mother. This routine goes on until my mother has had it with the lot of them and chases them all out with a wooden spoon. For every infraction I committed as a child, the wooden spoon was threatened. Not that she ever actually spanked me with it. She just chased my brother and me throughout the house, screaming in Italian.

The women all clustered around the stove. "Add more oregano, Rose."

"It needs a pinch of...something. Hold on...maybe some more garlic."

"Can't have too much garlic."

For my mother, the red stuff she slaves over is a religion. She has been known to actually break out in a cold sweat at the sight of a jar of Ragú. That's sacrilege of the highest order.

Lady Di and I always gather in the kitchen because it's what we do, feminism aside. The men watch football during the season, and with most of them heavy gamblers and bookies, it's either a joyous occasion or the cause of a lot of screaming. Either way, the language flying through the room would make Sister Mary Catherine of my old grammar school roll over in her grave.

Lady Di is considered an oddity, being as she comes from way across the Atlantic, and she had never even eaten true gravy before meeting my family, nor had she ever teased her hair, or even discovered the wonders of Aqua Net hairspray—the aerosol-can variety. I'm not even sure if the Aqua Net company still makes it, thanks to the ozone layer's problems. However, my mother and her sisters have enough stockpiled to take them into the next decade.

"Diana, honey, can you stand a little advice?" My aunt Gina cornered us in the kitchen. Diana had no time to answer before Gina, cigarette dangling from the corner of her mouth, was pinching her. I don't mean like a little pinch on the cheek, either. I mean she was pinching her upper arm for all it was worth—Lady Di showed me a bruise later. "You could stand a little meat on these bones."

"Well…I—"

"Honey…men don't like bags of bones. You wonder why you're not married? *This* is why." She stated this with such certainty, oblivious to Di's beauty.

"Actually, Aunt Gina—" I felt the need to defend my pinched roomie "—Diana has a lot of boyfriends, and she's been proposed to three different times. She's not married because she doesn't want to be married."

"Bullshit." Aunt Gina pinched her again. "Look at this. You see this, Andrea?" She motioned to one of my other aunts. "You see this? Both of them. Really, Theresa Marie, you, too. You think you're all fancy living off in that city, but when your uncle Rocky proposed to me, I was the babe of Brooklyn."

I stared at Aunt Gina and glimpsed, beneath the pile of big hair, the perfumed face powder and the sixteen gold-and-diamond necklaces she wore stacked around her neck like a snake's coils, the beautiful neighborhood girl she once was. I still love looking at old pictures of them, just as I loved looking at them as a little girl. I laugh when I see pictures of them all from back then, the girls in eyeliner and Pucci dresses—the first time Pucci was in—the boys in zoot suits too big for them. They all have highball glasses in one hand, cigarettes in the other. You can see the smoke swirled around their faces and can almost smell it, as well as hear the giggles and tough talk, mixing together as they lived "the life" then.

"I'm sure you were, Aunt Gina."

"I was. Ask your mother, Theresa. Ask her."

Lady Di humored her. "So come on, Mrs. Gallo, were you girls 'it' back then? The bomb?"

My mother usually waves off such talk with a flick of her spoon and a roll of her eyes. But her sisters wouldn't let it rest. "Come on…" Aunt Marie snuck up behind my mother and pinched her on the arm. "Tell the girls about when we used to go out in the city."

"Honey…" Aunt Gina gestured with her thumb toward the living room where we could hear screams and cheers erupting after various plays in the game. "They may not look like much now, those balding bastards, but way back when they were all catches, every last one of them."

My mother twirled around. "Theresa…every girl was in love with your father. But his family was considered trouble. He was a bad boy, you know. But underneath it, I could tell he was a real softie. Now, all of you—" she glared at the room full of us, packed tight around the table "—get outta my kitchen!"

We scattered—not before Aunt Connie reiterated for the twentieth time that the gravy needed both garlic and oregano. In the living room, my male cousins, three of whom are named Tony, clustered around Lady Di. She chose to sit next to the "hunky" Tony, who had staked out our apartment not three days before. His massive biceps belied the fact that I knew he liked nothing better than to cook pastry. He sometimes came up to our apartment and I taught him recipes. He was a fast learner. I know he liked being up there with Diana and me. Whenever he was around her, he stood a little taller, and he never cursed. He was an amateur chef in the making, but he'd never let the family know that. Pizza was one thing—maybe—pastry was another.

A half hour, and one Giants touchdown and an interception later, it was halftime and that meant we would shovel food in as fast as possible before the game resumed.

The first course was eggplant parmigiana, as well as a heaping bowl of homemade ravioli stuffed with ricotta that Ma got special from the Italian deli. Then she brought out huge bowls of gravy, teeming with large sausages, meatballs and whole lamb chops on the bone. This was served on pasta, also homemade. Garlic bread, a large salad, bowls of olives and plates of sliced pepperoni and fresh mozzarella, which, if you've never had it, has the consistency of congealed I-don't-know-what. It's beyond gross, wet and rather tasteless, but the Italian deli carries that, too.

And we were just warming up.

Later, a huge ham came out. Followed by a seafood course, including an Italian version of octopus, legs flopping over the side of the bowl, looking like they were trying to make a run for it. Through it all, as bowl and pan, and plate and platter made their way from the kitchen to the table and everyone started fanning himself or herself as the temperature in the house rose from the oven opening so often and boiling pots on the stove, my mother never sat down. She moved from kitchen to the dining room, back and forth, back and forth. She sat down occasionally, but watched over the table like General Patton, waiting for a movement of the troops that might signal we needed something, then she'd leap up and fetch it. Bottle after bottle of good red wine was opened. Forget letting it breathe. Around our house, a bottle of wine never sits still long enough to breathe.

I loved watching the insanity of it all. Sundays were sacred when I was growing up. I think that's why I ended up being a chef. I didn't go to culinary school. I was *raised* in culinary school, standing on a stool with a makeshift apron on—a towel tied in the back. I learned, as a little girl, that the way to my father's heart was through his stomach, and by the time the whole stereotype of the "little woman in the kitchen" was something to resent, I was hooked. The kitchen was where I felt content and happy; cooking was a way to relax, a way to create.

The men ate huge mouthfuls of food, occasionally grunting their approval. Poppy Marcello was especially happy with the sausage. Lady Di consumed five glasses of red wine and got giddy enough to ask Uncle Rocky to sing a Louis Prima song, then some Frank Sinatra. Call it the Marcello version of karaoke. We laughed and ate, but I noticed my mother wore a pair of house slippers and, not for the first time, I could see how Sundays wore her out, even when she wasn't hosting. But if I offered to help her she would turn me down flat. This was her show, just like, I guess, at my restaurant, the kitchen was my show. I hated when Quinn came back, lifting lids to pots and looking over my shoulder. "Go back to chasing the waitresses," I'd yell at him.

The women all rose and began clearing as soon as the game came back on. The men would take plates in front of the television for further eating while my mother readied dessert. At one point, Ma and I were alone in the kitchen.

"I wish one of these Sundays you'd bring home a man, Theresa Marie. None of us are gettin' any younger."

"I know, Ma." I rolled my eyes and tried to find room in the overstuffed fridge to put leftover eggplant. It didn't look like I'd fit a single black olive in there.

"I don't understand what's so hard. There are what, forty million men in Manhattan? At this point, I give up on you even finding someone from Brooklyn. Manhattan would be fine. Non-Italian would be fine. You can marry an Irishman. Hell, a nice Jewish boy. Just someone. A warm body, for

God's sake. Though Catholic would be good. Your father would like that."

"First of all, Ma, there aren't forty million men in Manhattan. Second, however many there are…forty percent of them are gay."

"Very funny."

"I'm not kidding."

She slammed down a pan. "You should move back home."

"I'd rather eat fifty pounds of scungilli and explode."

"Outta my kitchen!" She slapped my arm.

Moving back into the living room, I saw five of my cousins and my father on their cell phones. Placing bets, checking on the book they'd taken. The women were martyrs. The men were criminals. Me? I was just certain that I'd never find someone who would understand the dance of it all.

My father stood up to stretch. Sometimes he liked to go outside on the front steps of our house and smoke a cigarette. I saw him go out the front door, and I followed him.

"Hey Dad."

"Teddi Bear, come 'ere." He stretched out an arm and wrapped it around me and kissed the top of my head. "I come out here for a little quiet. Those women are like a gaggle of friggin' geese."

"I know…. Ma's giving me the 'hurry up and get married' speech again." I looked up at my father. He slicked back his hair in a pompadour and favored polyester shirts in ugly colors like lime green. He wasn't Manhattan stylish, but he was still handsome, his jaw square with a dimple in the middle, and his eyes nearly black and penetrating.

"She's kind of a broken record with that one."

"What about you, Dad?"

"What about me?"

"Am I this big disappointment because I haven't found Mr. Right? Should I marry some Brooklyn boy and live around the corner from you and Ma?"

My father smiled a half-sad, sort of mysterious smile. Then he took my chin in his fingers and tilted my head up so I was looking right into his eyes. "Teddi…when I first set eyes on your mother, believe it or not, I knew she was the one."

"Struck by the thunderbolt?"

"Not quite. The thunderbolt is like crazy love. We were just high school kids, you know. I was a player. She was the prom queen. But I knew what I wanted. I wanted a nice girl I could have babies with. A good cook. Pretty."

"And?"

"And don't tell your mother I said this or nothin', but that was then. This is now. I don't want to see you like my brother's kid—Angela. Divorced with four fuckin' kids to feed. You take your time. And who knows? You just might get struck by the thunderbolt."

"I hope not."

"Why do you say that?"

"Aunt Mariella and Uncle Mario."

He nodded. After my uncle Mario had been paroled, he married Mariella in Las Vegas two weekends later, and they never left Sin City. They never came to Brooklyn to visit. Too many painful memories, they said. But once, my grandmother and Poppy had gone to see them in Las Vegas, before my grandmother died a few years back. When they returned, my grandmother wouldn't speak about what they'd seen for the longest time. I found out what happened from my mother, whispering—which in my mother's case is more like what other people call a normal speaking voice—to my father one night, when they thought I couldn't hear.

Mariella, crushed by waiting for her true love all those years, had long since gone mad. She was no longer the beautiful woman from the picture in the photo album. Her beauty was still there, but her eyes, so fiery in the photos, were flat. She was extremely childlike—she wouldn't go to the grocery store by herself, or even cross the street. But my uncle Mario remained true to her, doing all the shopping, even cutting her meat for her and helping her do her hair. I suppose some people might think that's romantic in a tragic way. I just thought it was tragic. Period.

"You know, Teddi…it doesn't matter who you marry. I just want you to be happy."

"I'm happy in my restaurant, Dad."

"Yeah…but when you're old and gray, it's not like you can curl up next to a plate of spaghetti and meatballs, Teddi."

I didn't see the point in telling my father that was the stupidest thing I ever heard. I just nodded as if he'd told me the sagest wisdom a father can impart to a daughter.

He lit his cigarette, and I kept him company while he smoked it. Then we both turned to go back inside.

"You know, Teddi," Dad said as he pulled open the door. "I do just want you to be happy. An' no pressure or anything, but the reason your mother acts this way is that you're your mother's only hope. That brother of yours…he's dating a girl he met at the Playboy mansion this week."

"I know," I said, and rolled my eyes. Where my brother Michael was concerned, forget being struck by the thunderbolt. He was blinded by brainless blondes with boobs.

★ ★ ★

"I'm so full I could positively vomit." Lady Di clutched her stomach as she rocked slightly on the couch back in our apartment later that night.

"It's truly torture. It's a week's worth of calories. Sometimes I wonder if we shouldn't skip it once in a while." I was ensconced in our overstuffed living room chair—a descriptor that matched my own swollen belly.

"Oh, please, Teddi, your mum would have your uncle Lou here in ten minutes flat to check on us if we didn't go. It's simpler to go along."

"I don't know how you can be so blasé about it. Uncle Lou's like an oversize baby-sitter."

"Because they're not *my* family, Teddi. It's easier to find them slightly dotty and laugh about it."

"Well, I'm glad my world exists to amuse you."

"Don't be cross, Teddi. They really are sweet in their own way."

"Sure. *You* didn't have to hide the Career Day notices from elementary school. Every kid had his or her parent in to talk to the class for five minutes about their job. There were three cops and a bunch of firemen, a stockbroker, a lawyer or two, a doctor, a teacher…one kid's father owned a dry-cleaning business. Joey Antonelli, the plumber. There was even an out-of-work actor. Everybody had someone there but me. I mean, what was I supposed to do? We had twenty-two phone lines in the basement for my father's bookie business. I couldn't drag him in for Career Day. And then there's the fact that…well, I'm still not one hundred percent sure what it is he does. Bookie? Loan shark? Well, anyway, not Career Day material."

"I would have thought it would be very interesting."

I threw a pillow at her.

"I'm serious," she protested. "Think of all the little minds who could have been turned on to a life of crime. It's perfectly charming!"

"All I'm saying, Diana, is it's charming as long as it's not happening to you. But these Sunday dinners not only blow my diet, they're exhausting. I love my family members— each and every one. It's the constant harping on my lack-of-a-boyfriend status. If I have to hear one more time that we're both destined for old maid-hood…"

"Ignore them. Ignore them, Teddi. It isn't worth it. You need to become more like the British. Smile and nod. Smile and nod." With that, she sat upright, glazed over her eyes and began waving at me like a very stiff Queen Elizabeth, turning her hand just so, smiling and nodding as if greeting me from her gilded coronation carriage.

"Your father at least had a real job."

"Oh, please. His job is to sit around with a stick up his ass." I laughed. "Smile and nod, Lady Di. Smile and nod."

"Don't make me laugh, Teddi. I'll vomit, I swear. How is it you don't weigh four hundred pounds growing up in a family like that?"

"You learn to pick at your food and make it *look* as if you ate. I don't know…it's like the restaurant, I just taste everything and don't ever finish any one thing. Plus my family serves things like sheep's head. Did you try some of that?"

"No. And the sight of your gorgeous cousin Tony gnawing on a sheep's jaw bone—it still had teeth on it for God's sake—may have cured me of my infatuation."

"My father used to stack the heads one on top of the other in the extra freezer we had out in the garage. They're quite a delicacy, you know."

Lady Di shuddered. "They make me squeamish. Really horrid things. And that squid stuff…"

"It's an acquired taste."

"Still, all that delicious pasta… Even picking and choosing, I would weigh four hundred pounds. As it is I *starve* myself every Saturday so I can eat at your mum's on Sunday."

"Yeah…well, I carried a few extra pounds in high school. I've learned to keep it all in balance now."

I stood up and stretched. "I am so full I'm falling asleep in the chair. I'll see you in the morning."

"Right, love. Listen, I'm too full to move. Can you put on channel two on the tellie?"

I switched the television to her favorite Sunday night cop show and went to bed. I had heartburn—a deadly combination of my mother plus Sunday dinner. I popped a few Tums and changed into my pajamas. Staring at my reflection in the mirror in the bathroom, I practiced Di's smile-and-nod pose and mildly amused myself, despite all the aggravation I'd suffered. Then I climbed into bed and was soon fast asleep, dreaming of disembodied sheep's heads dancing a conga line around the dinner table.

chapter 4

"Is this Pussy Galore enough?"

On Thursday night, with exactly one hour to go before I had to meet Robert for dinner, I stared at Lady Di. She was dressed in a black cat suit and a pair of black stiletto boots.

"You look like a dominatrix."

"I was worried about that." She rummaged in her closet and emerged with a hot pink scarf, which she expertly tied around her neck.

"*Now* do I look like Pussy Galore?"

"No. You look like a dominatrix with a pink scarf."

"Hmm." She turned to her closet again. "That's not what I'm going for here."

She pulled out blouses and tops and threw them on her bed. I try not to look in Di's closet, or in her room for that matter. She lives knee-deep in laundry, and her dresser is just a jumble of cosmetics, most of them half-used and drying out with the tops off.

She pulled out a long black blazer and put it on. "What does this say to you?"

"I don't know that it says anything."

"No, it must. It must say I am ready for *Mission Impossible. Charlie's Angels.* Scotland Yard. All that."

"Okay. It says that."

"But you don't *really* think so."

"Di." I sighed. "Can we concentrate here? Every time we pull this stunt, it's a fashion crisis."

"It helps me get into character, darling."

"Fine…let's run through the plan."

"Check. I call you on my cell phone…earpiece, little thingy here attached to my lapel."

"Check."

"At 0800 hours, I take these little pastries down to your cousin Tony—"

"What? Di…no military time. And that would be 2000 hours, anyway. You always screw it up."

"All right then…at eight o'clock."

"Right."

"When you hear on your cell phone that he is sufficiently distracted, you slip out and head 'round the block to catch a cab."

"Perfect."

"Then you go off on your date with Mr. Tall, Blond and Handsome, fall madly in lust, make passionate love and live happily ever after."

"I'll settle for a second date. Without a contingent of Italians following me."

We went to the living room where a large white box of fresh cannoli perched on the coffee table, tied up with twine from the bakery.

"I don't understand—" Lady Di eyed the box "—why these little pastries are such an obsession with your family. It's a little perverse, if you ask me."

"They're an obsession because finding them fresh and really well made with ricotta cheese and chocolate chips isn't easy. Make them wrong, and they're soggy. You can't just get these anywhere. That box there is a thirty-five minute cab ride *each way.* Even the pastry chef at Teddi's doesn't do them this good. Now, Byron, he's a good pastry chef—"

"I live for his tiramisu."

"Yes. But he's not really Italian. His family is from San Francisco…and he says they adopted him from an unwed mother who listed Hungarian as her background. And as good as he is at tiramisu, somehow, some way, his cannoli end up…well, not up to the Marcello-Gallo family standards."

"But it seems to me that pastry and ricotta cheese shouldn't have anything to do with each other. It's downright unnatural, Teddi. Pastry and custard, maybe…pastry and chocolate, pastry and a nice caramel or perhaps some ice cream, but these I do not understand. Ricotta is slimy."

"It's as Italian as sheep's head. Trust me. You don't have to understand. All that's important is that, with the exception of a woman in a micromini with very big hair, my cousin Tony loves cannoli more than anything in the world."

"Should I change into a micromini?"

"No. The cat suit is sexy, but trust me, he sees you with a box of pastry from my third cousin Tessa's bakery in Brooklyn and he'll be in love."

Lady Di adjusted her cell phone earpiece.

"All this because you're the only granddaughter of Angelo Marcello."

" 'Fraid so." My Poppy Marcello had five daughters and one son. One of his daughters, my aunt Connie, wasn't able to have children. She and my uncle Carmine owned a pizza place and treated me like a daughter. My aunt Gina had five sons, always figuring this "one last time" she would have the little girl she dreamed of. After the last son, my cousin Frankie, she packed the crib up to the attic for good and decided to hold out hope for a granddaughter one day. My aunt Marie had four sons. Though Uncle Vito held out hope for an even five—for a basketball team—she'd had enough. My uncle Lou and his wife had three sons—including the hunky Tony, though their oldest son, Sal, died. My grandfather watched pregnancy after pregnancy result in male heirs— and what he wanted was a little girl, he told my mother when she married, to spoil rotten, and to buy fancy dresses and Madame Alexander dolls for. He wanted to build a dollhouse. First my mother had my brother. No pink dresses there. Then she had three miscarriages before I came along. My baptism was celebrated with a party—including an eight-piece band—for three hundred. Three hundred people!

I did get the fanciest party dresses and doll strollers that were more expensive than actual baby strollers. Poppy built me a three-story dollhouse—a turn-of-the-century town house he even rigged with electrical wiring to light up the miniature chandeliers. I had expensive dolls with wardrobes that rivaled the *real* Princess Di's. But eventually, when I outgrew dollhouses and dolls and crinoline dresses, I was left with one *very* protective grandfather who was determined to see me married off in the grand style that befitted the last virgin in Manhattan—which, of course, he believed I was. And my cousin Tony was, in turn, my keeper. This was because he did not have a real job, and in the words of the family, he was a little lost. I knew it was because, though he could hustle a pool table with the best of them, and liked to go to the track with all my cousins and uncles, he wavered on whether he wanted "the life"—the "family," and all that went with it…including, possibly, ending up in prison like John Gotti's son. So rather than give him a job with too much responsibility, he was assigned to watching me, and in general acting as a driver for his father, whose glaucoma made driving impossible. The old guys of the family…well, they were getting old.

"Okay," Lady Di said, "I'm ready as I'll ever be." Lady Di lifted the box of pastries. "Off I go." She dialed my cell phone as she stepped out the door of our apartment. I had a walking commentary as she went downstairs.

"Entering the elevator…won't be able to chat until the lobby."

As I listened to dead air, I threw on my black velvet swing coat and grabbed my evening bag.

"Teddi?"

"Yeah?"

"Entering lobby. The cute doorman is on duty tonight. Winking at him—"

"Stay focused on the mission at hand!"

"Sorry. Oh, this is so Cold War, so *On Her Majesty's Secret Service.* Staying focused. Mr. 12B just gave me a very sexy look. I'm walking. Can you hear my heels clicking? God, I love these boots. Walking…walking. Mrs. Melman from the third floor just gave me the evil eye. Like I'd want to hit on that flabby, balding husband of hers."

"Focus, Di!"

"Okay then…at the revolving doors. Time for you to come down to the lobby."

I dashed out the door, locked it, then made my way down to the lobby. I listened to my phone.

"Walking across the street. See your cousin Tony. Waving and smiling to him."

Now I could hear traffic sounds, cabbies beeping their horns, then muffled conversation and her replies to Tony.

"You must be simply starving out here."

Mumble, mumble from my cousin.

"Well…I *know* how you find these positively delicious. Just wanted to say hello and bring you a dozen… *No,* it was nothing. Nothing at all for one of my favorite, most favorite chaps."

Mumble, mumble.

"Oh…you like this outfit? Just threw it on…. You know, Tony, one of these days we have to go out for dinner and get to know each other better."

Mumble.

"Smashing, then. You know, you're looking terrific. You working out?"

Mumble.

"Tony…I'm a little cold just standing still here. Positively shivering. What do you say we take a walk around the block? Get the blood pumping."

Mumble.

"Grand!"

And that was my cue. I dashed out the door, much to the bemusement of the doorman, who, I think, was on to our

charade—this wasn't the first time we'd gone to such ridiculous lengths. I made a sharp left and raced around the corner for a cab.

Flawlessly executed. Or so we thought.

But it turned out that Di's pastry hand-off was to have
devastating consequences.

I plead an overflow of sake. The piping-hot liquid must
have, like some alcoholic Drano, busted through my brain's
tiny capillaries and rendered me stupefied. So stupefied that
I revealed more than I usually do on a first date.

Robert Wharton was dressed like a power player. Maybe
that was it. I was overwhelmed by his expensive suit and silk
tie, and his dimpled smile and flawless TV-teeth. His manners, as he pulled out my chair for me.

Or maybe it *was* just the sake.

"So do you have any brothers or sisters?" he asked, leaning in to better hear me, his face illuminated by a single candle in a Japanese-inspired lantern on our table.

I had been mid-lift of a delicious piece of eel on the ends
of my chopsticks. Oh, God, here comes the obligatory family discussion, I thought. I dropped the eel in the little dish
containing my soy sauce.

"A brother. Actor. He lives in Hollywood."

"And your parents?" His eyes were a cross between brown
and yellow, and he looked genuinely interested.

"Not much to say. Have one of each. So what other
kinds of food do you like to eat besides sushi?"

"I'm adventurous. Like all kinds of food. Italian's my favorite, though. Which makes us rather well matched, don't
you think? I did an Internet search on your restaurant.
You've gotten some really good reviews."

"Thanks. We've been lucky…no…that's not all true. It's more than that. We work really hard at it. You shouldn't have a restaurant if you're not prepared to put in the hours. Anyway, I do love to cook Italian food, but to be honest, I love Asian cuisine. I like adventurous foods, too. I've even tried the legendary, sometimes-deadly blowfish."

"No way."

I nodded. "Di, whom you met, had her father here on a visit and got us all invited to some investment banker's dinner party at the Trump Tower. The man had a private chef…and they served blowfish."

"You *are* brave."

"I was kind of terrified. But at least now I can say I did it."

"Well…no blowfish for me. I'm not that adventurous. But if you ever want a guinea pig for some of your Italian cooking, I'm your man…. So is your mother a good cook?"

I struggled to think of questions to get him off the family track. Until the family thing came up, we had not run out of things to discuss. We were both huge football fans. He liked the Philadelphia Eagles, and I liked the New York Giants. We both loved bad kung fu movies—for reasons neither of us could explain—and those old dubbed Godzilla movies. We both adored dogs and considered our childhood mutts our best pals; we'd both even had a dog named Pepper, though, technically, my dog's name was short for Pepperoni. We liked eating out, the crisp days of fall and Bruce Springsteen.

"Oh, you know…typical Italian mother. Good cook, yes. Like I said, when it comes to parents, I had one of each. A matched set."

"You know, 'one of each' isn't much of an answer, Teddi. If I didn't know better, I'd say you were dodging my questions. I'm a reporter, you know. I'm trained to grill unwilling subjects." He winked at me. Then he poured me some more sake.

"Well…what about your family?" I asked.

"If I tell you about mine, will you tell me about yours?" He said it slyly, sexily. He had taken off his jacket, revealing a dress shirt crisply starched but very well filled out by what looked to be a taut body. Di would have declared him "smashing."

"Sure," I replied. Of course, I had no intention of doing any such thing.

"My family is old Philadelphia. Main Line. Stiff, upper-crust and boring with a capital *B*. Do you know, my mother actually uses words like *droll?* And she talks through her teeth, like this." He affected a dead-on Main Line accent. I wasn't unfamiliar with this type; sometimes the odd trust-fund Upper East Sider or Central Park Wester would come into Teddi's. Quinn would suck up to their table perfectly, then mock them in the kitchen with his gift of mimicry. I hated this kind of person and couldn't imagine Robert coming from such stuffed shirts. I guess I prefer my father, with his shirts always smelling of cigarettes and Aqua Velva, and his basement craps games when he let me blow on the dice.

Robert continued. "I was off at prep school by the time I was fourteen. Parenting always seemed like an inconvenience to my mother—whom, I might add, I always called Mother and not Mom. I knew better than to *ever* interrupt her four o'clock martini."

"Doesn't sound very happy." I thought of my boisterous clan. I don't think anyone in our family had *ever* drank a martini. Or said "droll." "Fuck" was my father's favorite

word. And when the men were alone, that was followed by
"asshole" and "bastard." What does *droll* mean, anyway?
And prep school? I was lucky they let me move out when
I was twenty-four. And then only with my own Italian se-
curity detail.

"No...not terribly happy. Though, I suppose, it was all I
knew. It was all my friends knew. Disinterested parents who
took us on fabulous vacations—along with our nannies so
they didn't have to bother with us too much."

"Was there anything you liked, I mean *really liked* about
your family?"

"Well, it's taken me a while to see some of the good
stuff. They encouraged me in school, and I really have my
father's connections to thank for getting me in the door
at Global News."

"And you like what you do...?"

"Thrive on it. And though my parents aren't the most
demonstrative people in the world, in their hearts they
wanted nothing but the best for me. My grandfather made
his fortune, and his father before him made *his* fortune. And
my father inherited it all, but he did say to me that I should
go and do something on my own, not just follow in his footsteps. When I said I wanted to be a journalist, my mother
acted like I'd said I wanted to join the French Foreign
Legion."

I laughed. "And your father?"

"In front of Mother, he mumbled something about being
careful not to embarrass the family.... But in private? He
took me into his study for a cigar and told me to go for it.
He said his great-grandfather was a bootlegger who liked
to fly planes and had an affair with a ballerina—scandalous
way back then. My father applauded that I wanted to do

something on my own. Something different—and he said my great-grandfather would have approved."

"Good for you!" I lifted my little sake cup and saluted him.

"Now, fair is fair. You seem very mysterious, Teddi. What about you?"

I tossed back my sake. "I was abandoned by my family and raised by wolves."

"Must have made all the medical and scientific journals."

"In fact, I did."

He laughed and poured me another sake. And that's when my mouth opened and huge contents of my brain began spewing out. I plead, as I said, the sake. And also, something about the way he talked about his great-grandfather warmed me more than the hot sake. I sensed he would understand the sort of grudging love you have for a family of eccentrics and law-breakers.

"Actually—" I lowered my voice "—I kind of am from the Marcello family."

"Not *the* Marcellos?"

"Well, as a matter of fact, yes, you could say that. The. As in *the* Marcellos."

"Holy shit!" Robert leaned back in his chair.

I envisioned the date being over. It wouldn't have been the first time. But he surprised me.

"I never put two and two together. Your last name is Gallo. They're sort of known in the same…uh…you know the same sort of context."

"Yeah. When I said I have one of each…I guess you could say I have one Gallo parent and one Marcello parent. One of each."

"How do you like *that* for a journalist? They'll take away my master's degree for that bit of ignorance…. I just didn't think you were one of *those* Gallos. So I take it the Marcellos are your mother's side?"

I nodded.

"Here I am thinking a bootlegger is scandalous. So what was growing up like for you, Teddi? That had to have been hard at times."

"No. It was more like interesting."

"Come on…tell me."

"Well…imagine instead of taking you to the zoo, your father took you to the track. Instead of reading Dr. Seuss to you, your dad taught you how to read a racing form. And that you spent family vacations in upstate New York, the better to visit the federal penitentiary when your uncles got put away."

"I can't imagine…. I mean, did you know your family was in the mob?"

"No. I thought it was normal. I didn't know there was a word for it—the *mob*. The Mafia. I didn't know until junior high, really, when a girl I considered my best friend told me her father wouldn't let her come over anymore."

"Junior high. God, my junior high years were a living hell. Come to think of it, I hated high school, too."

"Exactly. I had braces, no friends and an older brother who tortured me by taking the heads off all my Barbies and reading my diary to his friends. When the one friend I *did* have dumped me, I was devastated. I went to the library and started researching my own family. I mean, the Internet was around, but not to the degree it is now. So I sat there with the old microfiche and found the headlines. Dozens and dozens of them. Men I loved, my adored and favorite uncles." I shook my head. "I wondered if all the laughter and togetherness had all been a lie."

"Had it been?"

"No. It was just that, at age twelve, I had the ultimate introduction into the world of gray."

"I don't understand."

"The world isn't black and white," I pontificated over the sake. "It's all shades of gray.... I don't expect you to understand. I mean, you're a journalist, so I'm sure your world is about rooting out the black from the white, digging until it's all clear and clean. But I learned a different lesson, and I learned it young." I took another sip of my drink. "And I guess until this moment, I didn't appreciate it. But there was some value to the lesson, even though at the time it was like finding out all at once that the Tooth Fairy, Santa Claus and the Easter Bunny were all in league with Satan."

"You mean they're not?" He smirked.

Something about him made me feel at ease. His sense of humor, his listening skills. The fact that he hadn't run screaming for the exit when I told him (later) the story about my uncle Vito sawing off the head of one of his enemies. It was all rumor, but I wondered, I told Robert. Uncle Vito seemed to seriously dig his hacksaw collection.

We talked until I looked at my watch and found, to my astonishment, that it was twelve-thirty in the morning. "I have got a hellish day tomorrow," I said. "Friday is our busiest night. I really should be going."

"Sorry, Teddi. I didn't even think about it...I get to sleep in. I go to the studio late on Friday" He signaled our waiter, paid the bill, and we went outside and hailed a cab.

The cabbie was driving around on a pretty chilly October night with all the windows open and his heater going full blast. Maybe he liked fresh air. Robert and I huddled together in the back seat but didn't tell the cabbie to roll the windows up. Maybe we were both grateful for an excuse to cuddle.

"I'm not even going to invite you back to my place," Robert whispered, his breath on my neck. "Much as I want to. I don't want you to think I'm some typical guy. I want you to trust me. But I definitely want to see you again. Okay?"

"It's a deal." I looked at him. He leaned closer and kissed me on the lips. I shivered.

"When?"

"When do you want?"

"I'll call you tomorrow. This was a great night, Teddi."

I instructed the cab driver to let me off two blocks from my apartment. Before I slid across the vinyl seats toward the door, Robert leaned closer and kissed me softly, perfectly, again. I opened the door and waved goodbye, and I intended to slip into the building unannounced. The cab roared away when the light changed green. The wind was picking up, and I felt a few drops of icy cold rain. All I needed to do was slip past Tony and I was home free. I walked briskly, pulling up the collar of my coat. As I turned a corner, someone darted toward me with an umbrella.

"Keep outta the fuckin' rain!" Tony snapped at me as he popped open a large black umbrella.

"You scared me." Nearly jumped out of my skin was more like it.

"Imagine how I felt, my cousin goin' missing on me."

"I wasn't missing," I hissed at him.

He just walked beside me, his jaw tensing and untensing. Where was Lady Di when I needed her?

"Good night, Tony." I smiled at him when we got to my building, trying to get him out of his foul mood.

He just grunted, closed the umbrella and darted across the
street to my uncle's Lincoln Town Car.

Tele-phone.

Tele-graph.

Tele-mobster.

I gave it until early morning before my entire clan was
buzzing with the news.

And before I was called to a sit-down with my grandfather over ditching my cousin.

chapter 5

Office Memorandum: United States Government
TO: David Cameron
FROM: Mark Petrocelli, Special Agent in
Charge, Federal Bureau of Investigation
SUBJECT: Wiretap report, Angelo Marcello,
Marcello's restaurant, Brooklyn, New York
DATE: Monday, October 10

7:10 p.m.

Angelo Marcello: Teddi! How are you, angel?
Theresa Gallo (Marcello's granddaughter):
Fine, Poppy.
Angelo Marcello: Look here, what do I have?
Theresa Gallo: Poppy, I'm getting a lit-
tle too old for the silver-dollar-from-
the-ear trick.

Angelo Marcello: I know. Indulge an old man.

Theresa Gallo: A hundred-dollar bill from behind the ear? Poppy...you're crazy.

Angelo Marcello: Take it.

Theresa Gallo: Poppy...please...

Angelo Marcello: You want to deny me a little happiness? Buy yourself a little something. Or you and Diana go out for a nice dinner on me. *Si capisce!*

Theresa Gallo: Fine, Poppy. I love you.

Angelo Marcello: I love you, too. So why you wanna gimme *agita?*

Theresa Gallo: I give you *agita?*

Angelo Marcello: Yes. Like you don't know...

Theresa Gallo: Here we go...

Angelo Marcello: It's true, Teddi. Why would you go out of your way to deceive your family when we only have your best interests at heart?

Theresa Gallo: Poppy, I don't expect you to understand this, but I didn't ask to be in the...in the *family,* if you get my drift.

Angelo Marcello: What do you mean? Everyone has a family.

Theresa Gallo: Oh...so this is going to be one of those days. You know what I mean, you wily old Italian. The...*family.*

Angelo Marcello: Teddi Bear, I'm surprised at you. Family. I'm an honest businessman. I'm a restaurateur.

Theresa Gallo: I know, I know. So am I. But in your case...a meatball isn't always a meatball. Restaurateur... And I'm sure Uncle Sonny is an honest waste-management executive.

Angelo Marcello: *Agita,* Teddi. You're so fresh.

Theresa Gallo: Yeah, well, it's a family trait.

Angelo Marcello: What is?

Theresa Gallo: My feistiness. I got it from you. But look, Poppy, seriously, I didn't mean anything by it. I just wanted to go out on one date without looking over my shoulder and seeing an entire contingency of overprotective Italians watching my back.

Angelo Marcello: (Sighs.) I never should have let you move to the city. And buy that restaurant. You're changing, Theresa.

Theresa Gallo: Of course I'm changing. I'm growing up. I am grown-up. I'm twenty-six, Poppy. And don't call me Theresa. I'm still your Teddi Bear. No matter how grown up I am.

Angelo Marcello: You got me wrapped around that little pinkie finger of yours. From the first time I laid eyes on you, a tiny bundle home from the hospital. All right. All is forgiven...on one condition...

Theresa Gallo: What, Poppy? Anything.

Angelo Marcello: You invite this young man to Sunday dinner. In two weeks.

Theresa Gallo: Poppy! No! It was just a date. Nothing.

Angelo Marcello: So you're used to dating meaningless men? Like it's nothing?

Theresa Gallo: That's not what I meant, and you know it. God, you should have been an actor. Or a politician, the way you twist words around.

Angelo Marcello: Twisting words. I never heard of such a thing. Teddi Bear, do we have a deal? I'm waiting. I'm a very patient man as you know...Teddi Bear?

Theresa Gallo: Fine. A deal.

Angelo Marcello: Come give your old grandpa a kiss.

Theresa Gallo: Fine.

Angelo Marcello: Good. Now, how about *gabagool*. Rocco!

Rocco Marino (Chef): Yes, boss.

Angelo Marcello: A head for me and...what do you want, Teddi?

Theresa Gallo: No sheep's head. I'll just take manicotti, Roc.

Rocco Marino: Very good.

Angelo Marcello: What's this? Another hundred dollars behind your ear.

Theresa Gallo: Poppy...you're hopeless.

Angelo Marcello: Have been...ever since I laid eyes on you, kid, I told you. Ever since I laid eyes on you...

chapter 6

"Do you think your cousin has ever killed anyone?" Lady Di and I sprawled across my bed drinking champagne and listening to her favorite CD, over…and over…and over…and over again. Which wouldn't be so bad if her favorite singer wasn't George Michael from his Wham! days. And for the record, Di was too young to have even *known* George Michael then, but it was still this oddball obsession of hers.

"Which one?" I asked.

"Which one what? How should I know who he's killed?"

"Who who's killed?"

"Speak English, Teddi!"

"I am! Which one?"

"Which dead body? I don't bloody know."

I sat up. "Di…I've told you George Michael is killing off valuable brain cells. What are you talking about?"

"Tony," she sniffed, and then suddenly dissolved into tears.

"Di." I rubbed her back. "Di? This is so unlike you. In

fact…you're scaring me. I'm sorry I snapped. You just weren't making any sense."

"It's not that." She sat up. "Have a hankie?"

"Toilet paper."

"That'll do."

I got up and fetched her a roll of Charmin. "Here you go. Now what's going on, Di? I've never seen you cry like this."

"Oh…" She waved her hand up and down as if willing herself to stop the tears. "Bloody hell!"

"What?"

She took some toilet paper and blew her nose. "Promise you won't laugh. Won't think I'm mad. As in the queen's English, crazy, not mad…not angry, but plain insane."

"Sure, Di."

"The other night, with Tony…we walked around the block three or four times. And at the end, he held my hand. And…I'm bloody over the moon for him. I wanted to invite him up here and— Well…put it this way, I couldn't sleep that night. Or since."

"Why didn't you invite him up? Did you think I'd mind? That he's my cousin? Did I mention he's my *favorite* cousin? Seventeen male cousins and he's the pick of the litter. I'd be thrilled for you. Really, I would."

She sniffled. "It's not that. It's…I don't want to fall for him if he's a murderer. Suddenly, as we stood under a street lamp, I was sure he was going to kiss me, and my heart was just pounding out of my chest. Me…Diana Kent, who was kissed by the second grade and lost her virginity the year they packed me off to boarding school—lost it to the school riding instructor. Me…heart pounding like a nervous schoolgirl. And I realized what it is you've been telling me all along."

"What have I been telling you along? That you're an impossible slob? That you can't even boil water?" I tried to make her laugh. "That your views on George Michael—who is gay, dear—border on sickness. You can't change him, Di."

"Shut up, Teddi. No...about how complicated your family is. Suddenly he wasn't just this beautiful, chiseled, rock-hard, funny, sweet Tony. He was someone who may—or may not—have killed someone. Did he? Don't tell me! I don't want to know! No... Tell me—"

"Di—"

"Don't tell me! See? I'm conflicted." With that, she blew her nose again.

"Di, he's not a made man, if that's what you're asking."

"Made of what? What the hell does that mean? How could I ask that if I don't even know what it means?"

"It means he's not a murderer. Not yet at least, though I can't make any promises about leg-breaking."

"Leg-breaking is acceptable."

"Glad you feel that way. Anyway, it means...well, I don't know what Tony's plans are. He more or less functions as my uncle Lou's bodyguard. They collect book. But after my cousin Sal died—"

"That was very sad."

I bit my lip. "I know. And after that, I think even Uncle Lou started to wonder if maybe he should encourage his two remaining sons to do something outside the family business. He set up Mikey with a video-store business. Mikey isn't the sharpest knife in the drawer, but what he loves, more than anything, are movies. He can tell you every single winner of the Oscars since the Oscars began. So he's out of the family business, and Tony sits on the fence. He's going to have to decide sooner or later, but if he wants to open a restaurant or a shop or a small business of some sort, my uncle will set him up. And if he wants to enter the *family* business, that's his other option. Everyone trusts him. He's loyal beyond belief. And smart."

Di blew her nose again. "I don't know what to think. Could I really be falling for him? Could I? Is that preposterous? Me?"

"Stranger things have happened, Di."

"Well…all along we've been flirting. Almost since the first time you introduced us. Remember when he visited us at college?"

I smirked, remembering we had all played quarters, a keg of beer in our bathtub. Di, never very good at holding her liquor, had thrown up in the toilet, and Tony held her hair back. And they say chivalry is dead. "Yes, I remember."

"And all this time, it all was rather…well, it was all a moot point because it was flirting and it wasn't *real,* if that makes any sense."

"It does."

"And now…I don't know. We were under the street lamp and looking into each other's eyes and I was a bloody goner. Completely in love. In lust. In like. I don't know."

"I think that's wonderful, Diana."

"He asked me out. For a week from this Sunday."

I groaned. "Well…that Sunday will be interesting, then."

"Why are you groaning? You just said you were happy for me."

"I am. It's just…" I proceeded to tell her about my "sit-down" with Poppy.

"So you're going to bring Robert to dinner?"

"I'm not sure if the guy can handle it."

"It does seem rather early, doesn't it?"

I nodded. "On the other hand, he seems to find stories about my family amusing. Now he'd get to meet the clan in person."

"There's something to be said for getting such meetings over with. That way you don't build them up into this enormous, nauseating, sweat-producing, sickening event."

"Thanks for the visual, Di."

"Don't mention it."

Di and I continued to lie on my bed, drinking champagne and talking about men. Or, more precisely, Tony and Robert. Then I found myself telling her about the sad, doomed love affair between Mariella and Uncle Mario. Di cried. It was then we pulled out a calendar and decided the vast majority of Di's waterworks were caused by PMS. The rest of it could be explained by the fact that, after hearing about Mariella and Mario, Di was beginning to wonder if the moment under the street lamp with Tony was her thunderbolt.

chapter 7

The next night, courtesy of the two hundred dollars my grandfather Marcello had miraculously "pulled" from my ears through his sleight of hand, I told Di I was going to treat her to a night out at a little French bistro on the Upper East Side. I opened Teddi's, cooked for the lunch crowd, and then handed off the kitchen to Leon. Quinn was, of course, with those Irish-Italian movie star looks of his, greeting each table and doing his usual superb job of making everyone who entered Teddi's feel like a big shot. After the lunch crowd slowed to a trickle, he and I sat at the bar for our good-luck sambucas. Restaurateurs—at least Italian ones—are a superstitious breed.

Quinn grinned at me, his blue eyes absolutely dancing—doing a damn *macarena*—as he handed me my drink. Quinn is my first cousin on my father's side of the family so we have the same last name. He has long black lashes, that by all rights—if there's any justice in the universe—should have been mine. But no. I have to apply five coats of L'Oréal's Voluminous in jet black just so you can see mine, and Quinn gets to bat his impossibly full lashes at every woman who walks through the door. His mother is Irish, Aunt Colleen, and she says a novena for our restaurant every day, praying that we somehow, miraculously, in New York City, where restaurants fail each day, make it.

"What are you twinkling about?"

He leaned on the bar, his smile infectious. "I met a girl."

"God, Quinn…you have more sex in a week than I have had in my lifetime, I think. I don't understand it. I do and I don't. I mean, yes, you're beautiful."

With that, Quinn turned around and surveyed himself in the mirror behind the rows of liquor bottles. "I have to agree with you, Ted."

I grabbed a cocktail straw and threw it at him. "Arrogant and beautiful." I waved my hands (Italians speak with their hands). If I had to sit on mine, I'd be rendered mute. "And you have the whole bad-boy thing going."

"And last night, I was a very, very bad boy."

"Please, spare me the gory details."

"I'm a gentleman. I don't kiss and tell—except to my best friend, cousin and business partner all rolled into one, Teddi Gallo. We should have been born brother and sister."

I rolled my eyes but smiled despite myself. It was true. Of all my relatives, except maybe Tony, I loved Quinn best. And though I was very fond of Tony, especially when he came over to make pastry or to hang out and watch TV with Di and me, sharing pizza and wine, it was Quinn who was my friend, my true friend. I told him nearly as much as I told Di. My brother, Michael, and I could barely stand in the same room without it leading to an argument. I'm sure that pained my parents, but Michael had left Brooklyn and never looked back. Sometimes I envied his L.A. life so far away from the family, and other times I thought he did it out of some sense of shame, that my father with his pompadour and my uncle Vito in his "guinea Ts" and hairy back weren't good enough for Michael. None of us were. I had wished Quinn was my brother for as long as I could remember.

"How about you, Teddi? You're gorgeous. And you never date." Quinn wagged his finger at me.

"I'm married to this restaurant. I'm either waking before dawn to open, pulling a double shift or closing. How you can close this place six nights a week and then go out and party…and *then* go and get laid, I have no idea."

"I'm young. And so are you. Sometimes you just have to burn the candle at both ends."

"I did have a date the other night. Went well."

"Oh?" He arched an eyebrow.

"But I'll leave it at that. Don't want to jinx it…. And shouldn't you be prepping for the dinner shift?"

"Not without my sambuca, cuz." He lifted his snifter, and we clinked our glasses.

Quinn had gone to the Culinary Institute of America, and I truly admired how he could walk into the restaurant and instantly spot if a single fork was out of place. He was able to do it all and in any condition—hungover, on no sleep, freshly rolled out of a woman's bed. He had the energy of ten people.

After Quinn and I finished our good-luck sambucas, I went home, dumped my chef's coat in my laundry basket— my coat, embroidered in red script with "Teddi's" on the left breast, was caked in red sauce—then showered and waited for Di to get ready. As usual, I told her we were supposed to leave a full hour before we actually were. I had tried, over the years, to analyze just what it was that made Di so late. I honed in on the fact that she changed a minimum of six times before any outing—even something as simple as going to the corner deli for a bagel.

The bistro I picked was intimate, and the chef clearly knew his sauces. I was having a hard time choosing an entrée.

"See that fellow over there?" Di asked me as she sipped a Campari and soda.

"The drop-dead gorgeous one?"

"That very one. I think he's stalking us."

"Why do you think that?"

"Well…this morning, when I went to get my usual bagel—and tell me, why can't you get a good bagel in London? What is it about New York that positively *breeds* good bagels?"

"They claim it's the water."

"The water? What kind of rubbish is that?"

"I'm serious. When bagel makers go to other parts of the country…same recipe. Same flour. Same ovens. Different water. The bagels aren't as good."

"Fascinating. Well, I ordered a salt bagel. I know I shouldn't have extra salt—bloating. You know…PMS. But—"

"Lady Di…can you focus? Why do you think he's stalking us?" I looked over the man in question. I took him for about six feet tall. Very well built and muscular, but not too much so. In fact, everything, from his haircut to his shoes, was screaming *"ordinary."* The kind of ordinary that would make him hard to pick out in a lineup. He was very handsome, with chiseled features, but I could tell he was trying to blend in.

"Well…I ordered my usual," she continued. "Well, not my usual-usual, which is a plain bagel, fat-free cream cheese, black coffee. I splurged for the salt bagel. And he was there."

"Where?"

"In Charlie's Deli."

"So?"

"And then, because I'd noticed him, I thought back to another day when I was at the grocery store, and I swear I saw him there. It jogged my memory. And now he's here."

"I think I know what's going on."

"What?"

"Well, there's one way to find out whether he's simply from the neighborhood and coincidentally showing up at all our favorite haunts or if there's something more sinister afoot."

"Sinister? So you *do* think he's stalking us."

"How do you feel about getting our food to go?"

"But we just got here."

"Do you want to know who he is or not?"

"Not that badly."

"All right, then, I have a different plan."

We ordered, and when our food came, I told the waiter that we had tickets to a cabaret show and would have to leave at precisely nine-thirty. I discreetly handed him the cash, pre-paying for our bill.

Diana and I ate. The waiter brought over the bottle of white wine we ordered. The more French wine Diana drank, the giddier she got over Tony. I thought about Robert Wharton. He didn't make me feel giddy. No one did, actually. Not that I could remember. Maybe that was what attracted me to cooking. It let me pour all my emotions into the pot and the saucepan. From the time I was a little girl,

I swore to myself that when I got older, I would never sleep with one eye open, looking over to wonder whether my husband came home safe and sound. I would never marry a mobster. I would never marry a cop. Two sides of the same coin. I would never be giddy. Giddy was just another form of the thunderbolt.

When we finished our dinners, the waiter brought back my change, along with two mints. I looked at Di over the flickering candlelight. "Here's the plan. We bolt."

"Bolt?" Her eyes were glazed slightly from the wine, and she suddenly started laughing loudly. "What are you talking about, Teddi?"

"A hunch. Now, listen…when I count to three, we leave this restaurant like we suddenly realized the kitchen was on fire. And we see what Mr. Tall, Dark and Suspicious over there does. If he suddenly gets his check and makes a run for things, then we know he's following us. And if he and his table mate—" I referred to the man whose back was to us, also with an amazingly perfect haircut "—don't flinch, then it's all a little serendipity. You got that?"

"Got it. I love all this intrigue. I'm channeling my inner Pussy again."

"Don't say that too loudly."

"All right…Octopussy."

"Okay, Bond girl, one…two…you have your purse and shawl ready?"

"Ready."

I gently lifted my purse into my lap from the floor. "One…two…three!"

We suddenly leapt from our chairs and hurriedly made our way to the door. No, we weren't subtle, but we *were* out to the sidewalk in fifteen seconds.

"Come on." I grabbed Di's arm and made a beeline for an ice cream shop three doors down and half pushed her inside. Peering out the glass at the street, I saw the two men from the bistro suddenly make their way out the door of the restaurant. They stood on the corner, looking first left then right. Next they made their way to an unmarked van and went around the back of it.

Di gasped. "They *were* stalking us. Not just one, either. Two rotten little Peeping Toms. Maybe they've been spying on us through our bedroom windows." Di shuddered. "It gives me the creeps. They're pervs."

"You're half-right, Di. It's a 'they' stalking us all right. But they're not working alone."

"Not alone? I have the screaming abdabs!"

"The what?"

"I'm terrified! What is going on?"

"They were feds."

"Feds? What the hell are feds? You know, I realize we both supposedly speak English, but I swear to heaven I don't understand you half the time. More than half the time."

"Feds. FBI. They have been tailing my family since… well, since long before I was born. And that haircut and those shoes…the one was a dead ringer for a fed. The van clinched it."

"But you don't have anything to do with the family business. You paid back your grandfather every red cent he lent you to start Teddi's. You and Quinn. That anal-retentive little tight-butt of an accountant you use made sure of it. So why would these fed-people stalk you?"

"I believe the FBI would call it surveillance, not stalking. And I don't know why me. Not yet at least. But it pisses me off."

"Oh, God, no. You with a temper tantrum is truly frightening."

"Come on." I grabbed her arm. We braved out into the nippy fall air. I started walking right for the dark blue van.

"What are you going to do, Teddi?"

"You'll see."

When we arrived at the van, I went around back to the double doors at the rear. I started banging on them with all my might. "We saw you, you bastards! Open up!"

There was no noise, no movement, no nothing from the van.

"Maybe we've made a mistake," Di offered. "Maybe they cut behind the van and then across the street. It is dark out."

"There was no mistake. The only thing missing from this guy was a bulletproof vest. And he probably had one on under his shirt."

"We know you're in there!" I screamed, and pounded on the van again. Luckily, we were in the Big Apple, where it takes a lot more than this to attract attention.

"We're not leaving!" I screamed again. Turning to Di, I said, "Listen, we're going to make it so they have to come out. You go to the front of the van and sit on the hood. Just climb right up on the bumper and sprawl back on the hood and front windshield. They'll come out eventually because they can't leave otherwise. And trust me, FBI agents drink a lot of fucking coffee. Mother Nature and sheer tiredness will work for us. They have no idea how stubborn the Marcellos can be when we're fucked with, and let's not forget the fact that I'm fifty percent Gallo. Besides, Tony is bound to come here soon, too. He and Uncle Lou know we went to that restaurant. They'll find us, and they won't be happy."

"See…your family does have all the fun. Now I'm fighting the fed-people."

"Feds. Just feds, Di."

"Feds, then. Is this an appropriate outfit for this sort of thing?" She looked down at her Jimmy Choo shoes and mini-dress. She wore a heavy velvet wrap around her shoulders.

"Well…it's not quite Pussy Galore, if that's what you're asking, but my God, if Tony sees you in that, watch out."

"Smashing!" She beamed. "All right, then, I'm off to the front of the van."

I leaned back against the rear doors of the van, making a mental note of the license plate to give to my cousin Tony.

"Damn!" Di shouted from the front of the van.

"What?" I shouted back.

"These feds of yours now owe me a four-hundred-dollar pair of shoes, Teddi! I broke my heel climbing up on the bumper. I could scream blue murder!"

And maybe it was the wine, but as I walked around the front of the van, I noticed that Lady Di was not sprawled *back* against the windshield, but had plastered herself, face front, to the windshield so that her breasts were smashed flat against the glass, creating a *lot* of cleavage. Those G-men were surely happy fellows.

I walked back to my post and leaned against the doors. "We have all night, assholes!" I shouted.

Finally, minutes later, my teeth chattering from the night wind, I heard the sound of the van doors being unlocked. I stepped back and out emerged the very handsome agent we'd seen at dinner. I found myself suddenly unable to think of anything to say, but luckily for me, he stuck out his hand and smiled.

"You got us."

I stared at his hand, certain I should refuse to shake it on principle, but next thing I knew, my palm was pressed against his palm.

"Mark Petrocelli."

"Teddi Gallo. But you already know that."

"Look…" He grinned with a crooked smile. "I think we all got off on the wrong foot here."

"You're tailing me. There is no right foot. What you're doing is just as wrong as whatever it is you think my family has done."

"Now, Teddi, you strike me as a very intelligent woman." He spoke soothingly. "You don't really think that, do you?"

"All I know is this little cat-and-mouse game you're playing here is bullshit. You and your friends need to leave my family alone. And now you've sunk to spying on me and my roommate. You want to tell me why?"

"Like I said, you're very intelligent. You'll figure it out. In fact, I bet you already know. Or if you don't, Diana Kent, who at this moment is freezing her ass off on the hood of our van, does."

"Diana!" Something about Agent Petrocelli unnerved me. I had forgotten about poor Di and her broken Jimmy Choos. "Di! You can come down now."

"Right-o!" she called out. "I'm coming."

Turning back to the agent, his hair trimmed to regulation-perfection, I snapped, "Why don't you go follow around the members of the Gambino crew? They're into a lot more shit than my family."

"What makes you think we're not tailing them, too?"

"Listen…I don't know what you think Diana and I know, but whatever it is, we don't."

Lady Di came limping around the corner of the van, half

hopping on one foot and holding out a very broken shoe. "You!" she seethed at the agent, "stop stalking Teddi. And you owe me for the price of my shoes. Who can I send the bill to?"

He smirked. It wasn't only his grin that was crooked—he had a very deep dimple in one cheek, and no dimple on the other side. Yet, this made him look boyish, despite his build and demeanor. "I don't know if Uncle Sam is going to buy you new shoes, Diana."

"And how do you know my name?" she demanded.

"Di," I answered before the FBI agent did. "*This* is where our taxes go." I pointed to Agent Petrocelli. "Welcome to the wonderful world of our government at work."

"It's not *my* government," she retorted. "In *my* government the most we have is a completely loopy royal family. Remember our infamous illicit tape recordings, with Prince Charles wanting to come back as that horsey-faced Camilla's tampon and things like Squidgy-gate? But we *don't* have big burly men frightening innocent women and causing them to break their Jimmy Choos!" And with this she shoved her shoe, hard, right into his chest.

I looked up at Agent Petrocelli. I expected that at any moment five more agents would come swarming out of the van and put cuffs on us both. Instead, still smiling, he reached into his jacket pocket, took out his wallet and handed me his business card.

"You send me a bill for your friend's shoes," he said, "and I'll pay for them out of my own pocket."

"I bet!" Di snapped. "You're probably all talk, no trousers."

Agent Petrocelli looked at me.

"Means she doesn't believe you."

"I'm completely sincere. Now, if you'll excuse me, ladies, I think since our cover is blown, we may as well call it a night." Looking right at me, he winked. "See you around, Teddi."

With that, he opened the van door and climbed back in. As they pulled away, Diana elbowed me. "Well, how do you like that?"

"What?"

"Agent Hunk is smitten with you."

"No, he's not." I offered my arm, so she could lean on me as we started back toward the corner to hail a cab.

"Is, too. I saw the wink."

"He had something in his eye."

"No. It was a wink."

"Maybe that's just his way."

"Well, he didn't give *me* his card. And *I'm* the one with the broken goddamn shoe. I could just cry. They were my favorite pair."

I looked down at the card in my hand—Special Agent In Charge. What did that mean? Did the FBI have un-special agents?

We got to the corner, and I shoved the card into my purse. "Listen, Di, don't tell my family about this."

"Why not?"

"Well, at first I thought we should, but on second thought, I think it would be better if we didn't. That would make my family even *more* paranoid. Speaking of which—" Out of the corner of my eye, I spotted my uncle Lou's Lincoln, with Tony at the wheel, careening over to the corner. He barely put it in Park before he was out the door.

"Diana! Are you hurt?" He looked down at her naked foot and assumed, I guess, that she'd sprained her ankle.

She glanced sidelong in my direction. It was up to me to concoct a lie. But I wasn't raised in the mob for nothing.

"She got her heel caught in a sidewalk grate. Twisted her ankle, poor baby."

Tony, muscular as a bodybuilder, lifted her into his arms and carried her over to the car. "Let's get you home and put some ice on that ankle."

"Right-o, Tony." She patted his chest and then leaned against him. "Working out, are you?"

I followed behind. He opened the rear of the car. It was empty.

"Where's Uncle Lou?" Diana asked.

I shot her a look. In my family, you learned early on not to ask too many questions.

"He had business to take care of," Tony said gently. He had to be in love with her. If I had asked something as naive as that, he would have snapped at me. But he said it to Diana as gently as a kindergarten schoolteacher explaining how to mix red and blue to make purple.

I slid in next to Diana, and Tony drove us home, then carried Diana through the lobby and up to our apartment. Setting her on the couch, he remarked, "Thank God, Diana, it doesn't look too swollen. Let's get some ice, though."

He went into the kitchen, and I heard him opening the freezer.

"Go help him," Di urged. "He doesn't know where we keep the plastic bags."

"I would follow him, but I'm in too much shock that he knows how to open the freezer door himself. He actually *is* a member of the twenty-first century." In all my years of Sunday dinners, I had never seen a male member of the family in the kitchen except to bitch that the women were taking too long getting food on the table. And though I knew Tony did like making pastries—in fact had asked me for recipes—he was hardly known for waiting on anyone. In my world, that was for the women. The men didn't clear their plates. They didn't make their beds. Even if they moved out of the house, they brought their laundry home to their mothers.

I walked into the kitchen, where Tony had, all by himself, figured out where we kept both gallon Ziploc bags and kitchen towels. He had her makeshift ice pack all ready. I felt like I was Dorothy, and I'd just stepped foot in Oz.

I went to the refrigerator and opened it. Typical refrigerator of two single women. Stacks of old Chinese takeout and to-go boxes from Teddi's. A jar of mayo. Twelve cans of Diet Coke. Four bottles of champagne. I pulled one out and uncorked it, pulled down three glasses from the cabinet and went into the living room, where Tony had Di's foot propped up on two pillows on top of his own lap, and was holding the bag of ice, wrapped in a dish towel, on her ankle.

"Champagne?"

Di nodded. "I could sure use a drink after tonight."

I stared at her, willing her to shut up.

"What happened tonight?" Tony asked. "You mean your ankle?"

"Yes," she recovered, and smiled, batting her eyes.

"I'll take care of you." He patted her knee.

I blinked hard at him as I poured three glasses of champagne. Tony was my closest cousin in age—twenty-seven. And he and I had grown up in the strange and colorful Marcello clan. He had tormented me when I was a kid, hiding my favorite doll, Verushka (having already tired of my unruly family as a child, I aimed to name my dolls something as far-flung and removed from Italy as possible), and playing monkey in the middle with me *always* in the middle. When my teen years arrived, he was only too happy to point out to all my boy cousins that I was wearing a training bra. And when I went through a slightly chubby summer, the year before ninth grade, he called me Porky.

We both went to college—not everyone in the family did. Uncle Carmine had put himself through night school to get a degree in business, but he was the only one of that generation, though two of my aunts had gone to Katharine Gibbs secretarial school. In my generation, most of the cousins were pool hustlers and bookies, and a half dozen worked for the Marcello pizza chain managing restaurants. My brother, Michael, started college but dropped out sophomore year. Only Tony and I had actually earned degrees. And Quinn, but he was from the Gallo side of the family. However, Tony and Uncle Lou ate at Teddi's three times a week for lunch—the Marcellos and Gallos all ate at Teddi's to be certain we survived. And over time Tony and I had developed a sort of grudging affection.

I sipped my champagne and looked at the two of them, cozy on the sofa. "You know, I think I'm going to go to bed."

"Don't, Teddi. Please…stay out here with us," Di urged. That was a trait I truly admired in her; even if she was interested in a man or had a boyfriend, she didn't pull the "I've got a boyfriend and now I have amnesia where my friends are concerned" act.

"That's okay. I'm really, really—" I affected a yawn "—tired."

"Good night, Teddi," Tony said a little too quickly.

"Good night, you two," I said, and turned to go to my

bedroom. As I walked down the hall, I could hear the faint murmurings of sweet nothings between my cousin and Lady Di.

I punched my pillow and kicked my covers onto the floor. I couldn't sleep. Every time I shut my eyes, I saw Agent Petrocelli's smirk, and I heard him say that Diana would know why he was tailing us. Nothing made sense. Most especially this strange feeling in my stomach every time I pictured his face.

I finally gave up on anything close to resembling sleep at one-thirty in the morning. I flicked on the light in my room and listened in the darkness. I had heard Tony leave around midnight. No sounds emanated from Lady Di's room across the hall. If she were awake, she would be listening to George Michael. Instead, I turned on the television for companionship.

Flip. Flip. Flip. I used my remote to move from channel to channel, until I found one of the many cable stations showing *Law & Order* reruns. I think it's federal law that one of the incarnations of that show must run 24/7 on some cable channel.

It was midway through the episode. So now the suspect was in court, being hounded by the prosecution. I hated the prosecution. Which is not to say I rooted for the criminal. I didn't. But the men in the "law and order" part weren't perfect, either.

Growing up, I lived in a world of television fantasy. Enough of my peers avoided me because of who my family was, and the ones who didn't were more apt to want access to things they thought I stood for—drugs and stolen property—than to want to be true friends with me. The majority of my Gallo and Marcello cousins were male and wouldn't have played Barbie dolls with me if someone was aiming a .45 at their testicles. So I felt terribly alone much of the time, no matter how surrounded by boisterous family I was.

Television was my companion, and I now see all my viewing was divided into two areas: law and detective shows and shows with white-bread families.

I watched *Law & Order, Magnum, P.I., NYPD Blue.* Even *The Rockford Files,* which ran in reruns on one New York channel. My mother had a crush on James Garner. It didn't matter to me whether the show was first run or an old rerun, as long as a cop or detective was on it. I was intrigued by the characters. What was different about them? What made them choose that side of the law and my family the other?

I also watched *The Brady Bunch, The Partridge Family, Growing Pains* and *Family Ties.* Would Michael Gross as Mr. Keaton hide shoe boxes full of cash in the attic? Would he have hollowed out Mallory's Raggedy Ann doll to hide stolen jewelry? I think not.

So I watched the shows as a way of seeing how the other half lived. I watched as Dian Fossey might have studied the apes. I didn't understand why I was so different. I watched with longing. I watched with envy. And it wasn't until I met Lady Di that I made a true friend (besides Quinn) to whom I could tell all my secrets.

I flicked on the light. Agent Petrocelli had no idea what I had been through. He also couldn't know how much my father and grandfather and aunts and uncles loved me. He couldn't know about our world because he was trained to hate it. I climbed out of bed and padded over to a shelf on my wall where a few trinkets and memories of childhood perched. There sat my Raggedy Ann doll. I lifted her from the shelf and held her to me. She smelled of childhood. Of a world a lifetime away. I lifted up her petticoat and there it was. Carefully sewn into her belly was a great, big scar where diamond bracelets and rings and Rolex watches had once been hidden. My father told me if Raggedy Ann was ticking, it would help me sleep.

"Poor Raggedy," I whispered into the night. I took her and climbed back into bed. On TV, the suspect was breaking down on the courtroom stand.

"The prosecution always wins," I told Raggedy. And sometime after the show ended, I finally fell asleep, my old rag doll clutched to my chest.

chapter 8

Tony must have tipped off my uncle Vito that Diana broke her Jimmy Choos, because when we next arrived for Sunday family dinner, stacks of the designer's shoes were piled up in my aunt Marie and uncle Vito's formal living room.

"These can't be real. Can they?" Di whispered to me, turning over a stiletto with a rhinestone strap in her hand.

Uncle Vito overheard. He pulled his chewed-on cigar out of his mouth and said in a voice like rough gravel, "I hear from a very good source that these, young ladies, are the real deals. Now, you two take your pick before all the *comares* arrive."

My family made a great distinction between Diana, an unofficial adopted daughter, and me—both "good" girls—and the big-haired "sluts" my male cousins occasionally brought home to Sunday dinner. At the moment, my cousin Vito Jr., whom we called VJ, and my cousin Bobbie were both engaged to women whose version of big Jersey hair would put the Adriana character in *The Sopranos* to shame.

Uncle Vito swept his arm toward the stacks of Choos. "Take as many pairs as you want, sweethearts," he said. Then he stuck his cigar back in his mouth and went to join the men in front of the big-screen television in the den.

"He can't be serious," Di said. "These can't be real. This would be the equivalent of—" she made a mental calculation as she ran her finger along boxes, counting them "—of…God…of forty-thousand dollars' worth of shoes."

"He's serious, and if you don't think that those hairspray addicts are gonna claim every pair they can get their acrylic-fingernailed hands on, you're crazy."

"Where did he get them?" Di asked me.

"They fell off a truck."

"Really? How lucky then that your uncle Vito spotted them. They could have been run over. These precious, glorious, ab fab shoes!"

I stared at her.

"What!" she snapped. Then I saw understanding come to her eyes. "Aah…I get it. Another one of your sayings. They didn't *really* fall off a truck, did they?"

I shook my head.

"Stolen?" she whispered.

I nodded.

"Really?" She eyed the stacks. "Are you morally opposed to wearing stolen shoes, Teddi?"

"No. I figure it's one of the few perks of being in this overprotective family. Besides, we can't really give them back…."

We went digging through the stacks, trying on dozens of shoes, until we each selected three pairs. Uncle Vito had even left us shopping bags, so we put our shoes in bags and went and put them next to our purses in my aunt and uncle's guest bedroom. While we were in there, away from the family, Di said, "He kissed me."

"Uncle Vito?"

"No, you sarky ass…your cousin Tony."

"Well, I would have expected no less from you. You're right, Di, there's some kind of…something…between the two of you."

"Yes. I'd say it rivals the kismet between you and the FBI hunk."

"Blasphemer!" I joked.

"What?"

"Di…let me make this abundantly clear." I placed both hands on my chest. "*Me,* Mafia princess. *Agent Petrocelli,* one of the supposed 'good guys' and a mortal enemy."

"But that's why it's so perfect. It's so Romeo and Juliet."

"It's so *stupid.* It'll never, I repeat…it'll N-E-V-E-R happen. So get it outta your mind." "Outta"—why did coming home to Brooklyn always bring out my accent I strived so hard to shed in college?

"I won't get it out of my mind because he is perfect for you."

"You said that about Robert Wharton—with whom I shared a fairly fabulous kiss of my own."

"Yes, Robert is fine. He's lovely. But the man with the badge and handcuffs…he's beyond divine. And there's something between the two of you. I saw it. I was there."

"Change the subject. How was the kiss?"

"In my top three."

"Who'd he dislodge?"

"He dislodged Jeremy Talbott, the actor. He may, in fact, move into the number-one or number-two spot. God…

Teddi…I turn to mush just thinking about him. I can't wait to go out on an actual date next Sunday."

"It'll be wonderful. And what about today?"

"Well…it's rather a pain in the ass, actually. I have to pretend limp."

I rolled my eyes. "The things we do for love."

"No, Teddi, dear, the things we do for the…*family*." She winked at me. My God, my roomie was turning goomba on me! "By the way, Teddi girl, do you think your aunt has any Pepto-Bismol?"

"No, why? Your stomach upset?"

"No," she shuddered, and looked a little green.

"Hungover?"

"No." She winced.

"What then?"

"I promised Tony I would try a little lamby head today, and I thought I'd better be prepared."

"Gross!"

"I know. But I draw the line at the eyeball."

"Good for you."

"I keep thinking of 'Mary Had a Little Lamb.' The cute little lamby followed her to school, Teddi. That nursery rhyme said nothing about beheading the poor little thing and eating its eyeballs."

"Stop thinking about it as a…live little lamby. You'll never be able to try it then."

She shuddered. "Here goes nothing," she said, and turned and limped out to the kitchen where the women gathered over the weekly gravy.

I wondered, as I saw her later, closing her eyes and tasting the sheep's head, whether Robert Wharton would try an eyeball for me.

★ ★ ★

The next day, the thought of eyeball-eating briefly popped into my mind when Robert Wharton called me at Teddi's in the middle of the lunch rush. He had called the day after our date, but conflicting schedules had intervened.

"Hello, beautiful," he said. "I am so sorry that I haven't called again until now. I've been following that triple murder out on Long Island—the guy who killed that family because he was secretly obsessed with the mother."

"His dental hygienist?"

"Yeah, that one. I swear this job gets to me sometimes. Anyway, I had a really great time on our date."

"I don't mean to sound distracted…I, too, had a wonderful time the other night," I said, phone resting on my shoulder, "but I have three saucepans going and a table for ten out front."

"Sorry. Really sorry, Teddi. I didn't think of the rush. Can I call you at home?"

"Sure. Listen…I'll be up late. Tonight I close. I wouldn't be able to talk until the wee hours. You ever up at midnight?"

"Sure. I'm a night owl myself."

"Great." I gave him my number and promised to speak to him that night.

He called at 12:01. God, this guy was a gentleman who kept his word.

"Hey, Teddi." He spoke softly, in sort of a bedroom voice.

"What are you doing?" I asked him.

"Lying on my bed in my boxers—just in case you were going to ask if I was a boxer or briefs man—and thinking of you…. And what are you doing?"

"To be honest, having a sambuca. I worked a double and

am so wound up. Part of the dangers of working in the restaurant business. We get this adrenaline rush. Me and Quinn
are hooked. We love it."

"Who's Quinn?"

"My cousin. We own the restaurant together."

"So what are you wearing?" he asked teasingly.

"You naughty boy… Well, if truth be told, a big old
T-shirt. Not terribly sexy, I'm afraid."

"Now, there you're wrong. All wrong. There is nothing
sexier than a woman in a man's shirt, no underwear, with
that sort of just-rolled-out-of-bed hair thing going on. Half
sleepy. No makeup."

"Well then you'd be in heaven. The restaurant biz can be
murder, and that is often my very look. Especially the bed
hair. Can't say you'd find my typical at-home attire on the
pages of *Vogue*."

"*Vogue* women are overrated. I like real women. I like
you."

"I…like you, too."

"So when can I see you again?"

"Wednesday is the next chance. Just the lunch shift that
day."

"Wednesday it is. Good night, sexy Teddi."

"Good night, Robert."

I hung up the phone. No makeup. Rolled-out-of-bed
hair. I felt the rat's nest piled into a scrunchy on top of my
head. This guy could be a keeper.

Quinn was merciless.

"So who is this guy?"

"Shut up, Quinn. I just want to make sure I get out of
here on time today."

"Oh, no, sweet partner. Not until you tell all."

"All right then. He's a TV guy."

"As in repairs TVs?" Quinn, dressed in a fashionable black Versace shirt and pants, stolen by his brother who had, he'd told us the previous week when he came in for dinner, hijacked a truck in the garment district, looked aghast.

"No, you status hound. Not that there would be anything wrong with a TV repairman. It's an *honest* living." When Quinn and I opened Teddi's, having had this crazy dream for years (we designed menus in high school) we each took out on-the-books loans from our grandfather Gallo, my Poppy Marcello and Quinn's grandpa O'Reilly on his mother's side. And I insisted we pay it all back—something we were still doing after two years. Poppy and Grandfather Gallo were completely repaid by both of us, but his grandfather O'Reilly still had a hefty IOU. His grandfather's many businesses were legitimate, however, and the terms of the loan were generous. Quinn, on the other hand, who definitely went to the Belmont Raceway a little too often for my taste, would have done all our deals illegally. It seemed that everyone I knew believed in cutting corners.

"You looking for honest, Teddi? Why not date a garbage man?"

"That's exactly what half of the Marcellos claim they do, Quinn. But no…he's a TV guy, as in on the air."

"No shit. An actor? What show?"

"Not actor. News. GNN. He does on-air investigative pieces."

"I never watch the news, though that's very cool, little cuz. You fuck him yet?"

I rolled my eyes. And though, I suppose, Quinn sounded

crass, no one, other than jealous boyfriends of women he
stole away, ever got mad at him for long. It was his grin, his
whole aura, as if he knew a joke the entire world wasn't let
in on yet. People liked being around him. He gave off an
energy and shared it with anyone in his vicinity.

"What's his name, at least?" he asked.

"Robert."

"Bobby, eh?"

"No. Robert... Why is it all Italians shorten everybody's
name? Joseph becomes Joey, Robert becomes Bobby,
Charles becomes Charlie and Louis becomes Louie. His
name is Robert. And so long as we're talking, the new waitress is very good. She handled the lunch crowd Saturday as
if she'd been working here since we opened. Everyone
loved her. So—" I tried to give him my most serious look
"—do not...I repeat...do *not* fuck her."

"Cammie is gorgeous. Blond—"

"We haven't had a brunette work here since Christmas
of last year."

"—and delightfully perky, but not cheerleader perky. She
has just the right amount."

"Of perk?"

"Yes, of perk."

"The right amount?" I slammed down my knife, startling
Chef Jeff—not really a chef, but a young kid anxious to
learn the restaurant biz—who was lugging in large cans of
tomatoes.

"You've fucked her already, haven't you?"

"I didn't say that."

"You didn't say that, but I can tell. I've been able to tell
since you were fourteen goddamn years old, Quinn.
God...pretty soon there won't be a waitress in New York

City who hasn't worked here and quit. Which may be just as well—we can then hire only male waiters and stop with the soap opera up front."

"This one could be a keeper."

"None of them are keepers, Quinn. Because you can't *keep* it in your pants."

"You have no faith in me, your favorite cousin." He came over to me and kissed my cheek.

"You shouldn't come near me when I have a knife in my hands."

"I promise...I swear...this time I will not fuck this up."

I just shook my head and went back to chopping scallions. "You know Quinn, I've known you too long. It's like the ponies. You can't stay away."

"Blame it on my upbringing. But you still love me."

"Yes, I do. Blame that on mine."

Robert and I met at a restaurant in Little Italy. He had chosen a place right out of the movies. I felt like Robert De Niro in *GoodFellas* should have walked in. It was totally authentic. There were no menus. The waiters came over to the table and recited the night's offerings in Italian.

I gave up all hope of privacy, however. Not only did my cousin Tony park outside the restaurant, but I spotted Agent Petrocelli in the bar. He gave me a wink (again!) as I walked past him, and I nearly tripped in my heels. Robert offered me his arm.

"You okay, Teddi? Lose your balance?"

"Yeah. New shoes." I smiled. Looking back over my shoulder, I glared at Agent Petrocelli.

"Very sexy shoes, I might add."

Over dinner, Robert and I picked up where we left off.

The conversation never lagged, and he had an uncanny ability to make me laugh. After we ordered our dinner—a pasta marinara for him and a seafood special for me—he reached across the table and squeezed my hand.

"I have big news."

"What?" I asked excitedly.

"I've been asked to join the *Jerry Turner* show on GNN as an associate producer and on-air talent. I'll get to pick and choose my own stories, produce them. The sky's the limit from here. Think of the exposure. His ratings are number one on cable in his time slot."

"Congratulations," I said, because that was the appropriate answer when the man you are dating tells you about a big promotion. But the *Jerry Turner* show, I have to confess, was one step up from the *Pond Scum Show* in my book. Turner thrived on controversy, and if he couldn't find any, he delighted in creating some on his own. His favorite technique appeared to be the "blindside." He would invite guests to be on a segment, and then, in front of a live camera, he would suddenly turn on them and make them look like assholes. Every few weeks, he also did a really big, really tasteless, show…some kind of ratings-grabber. Like college girls working their way through school as prostitutes.

"This could be very big for me."

"Don't you find his show a little…"

"What?"

"A little…oh, I don't know, a little scandalous? A little over the top?"

I held my breath. I really liked Robert, and I wasn't looking to have our first argument. But he smiled at me and squeezed my hand again. "I'm a big boy. Yes, there's a little…more of that kind of stuff than I'd like, to be sure.

Come on, you're looking at the boy raised on Main Line politeness. But face it, Teddi. Without journalists like Turner shining the light in the darkness, where would we be? Look at Watergate. Look at all the good journalists do. If we have to go for ratings once in a while, it's just a sign of what the public wants. Regardless, Teddi, I plan on playing by the book."

"Well then, I guess we should be celebrating. Good for you!" I lifted my glass of red wine in a toast. He lifted his, and we clinked glasses.

"You look beautiful tonight, Teddi."

"Thanks." I had borrowed another elegant dress of Di's by a Japanese designer I had never heard of, but whom Diana had discovered in a fashion magazine and then pestered her father to ship back on yet another trip of his to Japan. Frankly, though she complained about her "veddy, veddy" British upbringing, I was willing to guess that in his own stiff way, Mr. Kent, earl of something or other, was wrapped around his daughter's finger, just as my father and my Poppy were wrapped around mine. The bonus? In my family, Jimmy Choo shoes and fake Rolexes. In hers? Dresses so expensive one barely dared to sweat in them.

"So does this restaurant feel like home to you?"

I looked around at waiters bustling out of the kitchen with heaping plates of pasta. "Very much like home."

"I'll have to come in to Teddi's. I wanted to go there for lunch today, but I didn't know if there was…I don't know, a protocol for showing up when the woman you like very much owns the place. I worried maybe you don't like cooking for people you know."

I looked across the table at him, melting a little. "That is really so sweet. I don't think anyone else has ever thought of how I might feel in that situation. It is kind of weird when people I know come in. Not family—they come in all the time, and tip big. I think they're convinced if they don't eat there that Quinn and I will starve. But it does feel weird sometimes when an acquaintance or friend drops by. I feel more pressure in the kitchen. Anyway...Teddi's isn't authentic old Italian. It's more a New York bistro. Romantic. Classy. Though in the bar, there's a nod to the Old World and Quinn's and my families."

"What's that?"

"Well, the main dining room we had faux-painted, and there are fresh flowers on every table, that sort of thing. But in the bar, we have old black-and-white pictures of both our families in frames, hung so close together there's barely any wall showing. There are pictures of our parents and our grandparents. There's a picture of Ellis Island. A picture my grandfather took of the Statue of Liberty the first time he saw it."

"I can't wait to see the pictures. The whole place. I guess that's why I chose this restaurant—truthfully I asked around at work. I wanted to take you someplace you'd love."

"Well, this place is terrific. My father would feel right at home here."

He laughed. "What is your father like?"

"Oh...Dad is kind of hard to explain. He's obsessed with sports—for gambling reasons. He's loud. A little gruff. He's terrified of my mother, and at the same time they go toe-to-toe. He likes to pretend he doesn't hear her, so growing up, his face was always buried in the racing sheets and the newspapers. He didn't talk much. I think he had an allotted word requirement of twelve a month. If I called home from college and he happened to answer the phone, he'd say—" I lowered my voice to affect my father "—'Hi…let me get your mother.' Note that was six words. He said it twice a month when I caught him on the phone and we were at twelve."

"I bet he's a softie underneath it all."

"Oh, absolutely. When I was fifteen and my appendix almost burst, he drove me to the hospital, didn't want to wait for an ambulance. Then he visited a church for the first time since his wedding day and said confession and six rosaries. The surgery was cutting it close. They thought my appendix might burst right on the table, and the recovery was none too fun. My father, they tell me, never left the hallway outside my room. Not once. He didn't come in to see me, either—at least not when I was awake—but I sensed his presence out in the hall. Sort of like a rottweiler guarding his family…. Now that I'm older, he and I talk a bit more. I'm his princess."

"And your mother?"

"Annoying. Overbearing. Big hair. Big heart." Out of the corner of my eye, I could see the sneaky Agent Petrocelli watching us over his glass of…I guessed club soda.

"Robert, I'm going to the ladies' room." I stood. As I left my seat, he rose out of his seat. Manners. I liked a man with manners.

Walking back to the bar area, I stopped right in front of Agent Petrocelli.

"Stop following me around."

"What makes you think I'm following you?" He played with the cocktail straw in his soda.

"Look, keep this up and I'll—" I stopped. I'd what? Call the cops? Make sure he slept with the fishes? What?

"Look…I'm just doing my job, Teddi."

"Don't call me Teddi. That's what my family and friends call me."

"I know. You're Grandpa Marcello's Teddi Bear."

"You fucking bastard." My voice trembled, and I could see the customers near us leaning in and listening attentively.

"Look…I have a job to do. And so do you, apparently."

"Fuck off." I turned to go, heading toward the ladies' room. My back was to him when he said the words that would wake me in a cold sweat for days to come.

"Did you know your pal, Diana Kent, aka Lady Di, is very close to having her green card revoked?"

I turned. "Are you threatening me?"

"No. Just stating a fact."

I felt dizzy. Diana was my best and only true-blue friend. I couldn't even picture my world without her. And what about Tony? He would be devastated. Maybe I had been wrong in not telling Poppy about the FBI tailing us. He could fix something as simple as a green card. Couldn't he? How many politicians did he have in his pocket? I took a deep breath. "Keep away from her. From us."

"I'd like to, but that package she passed off to your cousin Tony two weeks ago makes that impossible. You might want to think about talking to me, Teddi. Off the record, of course. I'd hate to see your friend shipped back to rainy old England."

The restaurant swam round me. I couldn't think. I couldn't breathe. So I did the only thing I could think of. I grabbed a drink on the bar and threw it in his face.

"Va fa napole."

Go to Naples, Agent Petrocelli. Go to hell.

chapter 9

If sleep was difficult before, it was impossible now. Every day, I half expected immigration officials to come pounding on our apartment door and haul Diana away. What did Agent Petrocelli mean by "revoke" her green card? I racked my brains trying to think of the best plan to keep her here, and more, I tried to figure out what the hell this FBI agent was so fired up about.

On Friday night, Di had decided to stay home and nurse a slightly sore throat. When I got home at twelve-thirty in the morning, she was waiting with champagne, had turned on George Michael full blast (much to my musical chagrin) and ordered take-out Chinese. The joys of New York City. Chinese takeout at one o'clock in the morning. We ate, cross-legged on her bed, as she kept getting up to clean her closet and decide on just the right outfit for her first official date with Tony on Sunday.

"Robert's coming to dinner, too, you know."

"That's right! I completely forgot. Let's go on a double date after dinner. It will be so much fun."

"No. Too high school. You go on your first real date with Tony."

"Is your Robert ready for Sunday dinner with all those Marcellos hovering around him?"

"Please. No man could be ready for this. But I asked him over to dinner because Poppy Marcello made me an offer I couldn't refuse. Robert said he'd be—and I quote—'delighted' to meet my family. Personally, I feel like it's too soon."

"Well, I'm sure they'll love him. Intelligent, handsome, smart and now a producer."

"He's also as WASPy as they come. He may faint when the heads come out."

"Give him a little credit. If I can eat lamby brains, he can. It's like that show. What's it called?"

"I have no idea. There's a show with lamb brains on it?" I actually got to watch very little television beyond the late-night talk shows and *Law & Order* reruns. I thought of getting a TiVo until I realized I didn't even have the time to watch taped TV.

"What the hell is it called? Oh, yes. *Fear Factor.*"

"What do they do? Terrorize people?"

"Mmm-hmm. They make them eat disgusting things."

"Like lamb's head?"

"No, worse. Live maggots and raw cow testicles."

I looked down at my Chinese food. "That's disgusting. Can we not talk about this?"

She put down her chopsticks and moo goo gai pan, and went back to her closet. "What do you think of this?" She held up a black-knit sweater dress by Calvin Klein, which I happened to know looked terrific on her.

"Good choice," I said without much enthusiasm.

"Teddi? What's wrong?"

"Nothing's wrong."

"There is something wrong. I can feel it. I can see it. Something's been on your mind since your date with Robert. When I stopped in for early supper last night, Quinn said he thought you were lovesick."

"Please. Quinn doesn't know what he's talking about."

"It's a shame he's such a slut. He really is delicious."

"Quinn? Yeah. You are the only beautiful woman since puberty to turn him down flat, you know. He considers you the Mount Everest of conquests."

"I know. He's always so utterly well mannered when he thinks I am watching him. When he doesn't, he's up to his old tricks. 'Can't teach an old dog,' that sort of thing. But I'm afraid this is one mountain the very good-looking Irish-Italian charmer will not climb, if you catch my meaning. Meaningless sex…no longer for me. I like a little substance there. Quinn is a playboy through and through."

"I hear he's unbelievable in bed. The waitresses compare notes at work. You would think they were talking about the Dalai Lama or something."

"What the hell kind of analogy is that? A holy man of sex? Please. Just because Quinn may know where a G-spot is doesn't make him good in bed. It takes more than technique."

"Oh, trust me. He has more than technique. He makes every woman feel beautiful."

"So are you?"

"What? Beautiful?"

"Oh, of course you are. Why do you ask?"

"Di…focus once again. What are you talking about?"

She thought a moment, lifted her chopsticks, then found her train of thought. "Are you lovesick?"

"No, Di, I am not. I like Robert, but you know me. I'm a little cautious... Hey, do you happen to know...if you married my cousin Tony, would that automatically make you a U.S. citizen?"

She laughed, putting down her food to go pull out her scarves and start to sort them. "No, silly. Besides, I like being an English citizen. Even if we Brits can't make good bagels. And who's talking marriage?"

"No one. I just wondered. I can't imagine if you ever went back to England, Di. I need you."

"Well...I need you, too, silly girl. But I don't plan on departing on the *QEII* anytime soon." She looked thoughtful. "Something's wrong, and I know just the cure for what ails you. Back in a jiff."

She dashed out her bedroom door, leaving me to stare at her open closet, clothes thrown on the floor in haphazard piles. No matter how much organizing she did tonight, it would be a mess inside of three days. I wondered what my cousin would think of a woman who thought gravy was something brown you put over turkey and mashed potatoes and wouldn't know how to clean a house if her life depended on it; Di was a stark contrast to his own mother, Aunt Tess, who seemed to go through life wearing thick, yellow rubber gloves with a bottle of Formula 409 strapped to her hip.

"Here we go." Di practically sang as she floated back through the door with a pair of cannoli perched on a plate.

"What's this?"

"I bought another box of these pastries for Tony. I'm not saying he's spending the night on Sunday, but just in case, I wanted to surprise him."

"Di...these will be soggy and disgusting by Sunday, let alone Monday morning."

She looked crestfallen. "Damn. Will they? I know...I'll trot on down to the car and bring them to him tonight. He must be there." She walked across the hallway to my room and peered out the window. "There he is!"

Coming back, she pulled a sweater out of her closet. "I won't be long. Why don't you eat one while I'm down there?"

"Sure thing. Italian pastry and chicken and cashews. What an inviting combination."

"Washed down with champagne, don't forget! Besides...is there *anything* that really goes with these god-awful, half-sour pastries?"

I shook my head. "Hang with Tony long enough and he'll have you eating them with little lamb heads for lunch every day."

"God, you are a sick girl.... I'll be right back." I heard her walk down the hall, fuss in the kitchen and then exit our apartment.

I stared at the cannoli. They weren't as authentic as the ones I dragged home from Brooklyn, but they didn't look half-bad. I stuck my finger into the ricotta and brought it to my mouth. A chocolate chip perched precariously on the tip of my index finger. Delicious.

And then, mid-bite, I had a revelation.

The box of cannoli.

The hand-off to Tony.

I stared at the pastries on the plate. That was what Agent Petrocelli saw. Or thought he saw. Di delivering a package to Tony. Could our little ruse to ditch my cousin the night of my first date with Robert now mean Diana would be sent packing across the Atlantic?

I stood and walked into my room. I found my purse and fished out the card for Special Agent Petrocelli. The man I'd thrown a Scotch and soda on.

I had two choices. I could either convince Mr. FBI that Diana was completely innocent, even as she now made happy plans to date my cousin, or I could tell Poppy Marcello everything and watch as he made me pack up all my belongings and move back home to Brooklyn.

With trembling hands, I picked up the phone and dialed the number Mark Petrocelli gave me.

Feeling like a secret agent myself, I made plans to meet Mark Petrocelli in Central Park.

While Diana was still sound asleep, I bundled into a jacket on Saturday morning, threw a scarf around my neck and hailed a cab to leave me at the carousel in the park. My cousin Tony only watched over me in the evenings— when, in Poppy's mind, killers and perverts roamed the city like wild jackals—so I was certain no one had followed me. I wore sunglasses, channeling, as Di would put it, my inner Pussy Galore.

Mark Petrocelli was pacing by the carousel. Even though his back was to me, I knew it was him. My heartbeat quickened, and I willed it to slow down, practicing my yogic breathing. A lot of good it did me. My nerves got the better of me, anyway, and my teeth chattered involuntarily. To top things off, I could feel myself blushing. Why did he have to be so good-looking? Why couldn't he be doughy, balding, with bad teeth and pockmarks?

I walked over to him and cleared my throat.

"Teddi." He smiled as he spun around. "Good morning!"

Wind whipped my hair around my face. "Can this be an off-the-record conversation?"

"Sure. Let's walk."

We strolled side by side through the park, to anyone else looking like lovers who'd met for a Saturday walk.

"Look…you have to believe me. Di and I have nothing to do with the family business. You need to stop following us."

"If you have nothing to do with the family business, why are you so important that you have a bodyguard?"

"I don't."

"I see your cousin Anthony and your uncle Lou outside your apartment at all hours. I've seen a few things, Teddi. You also happen to own a largely cash business, a restaurant. In a family that…let's just say might—just maybe—have an interest in laundering money."

My restaurant. That's what had gotten them interested in me in the first place.

"My restaurant is squeaky clean. You can bring a van full of IRS agents to climb up my ass, but I am telling you, they won't so much as find a penny out of place. My accountant is not a family accountant. He is an anal little man with a Harvard degree and a nervous penchant for chewing on the ends of his pencils. If he even *hears* the word *Mafia* he breaks out in a cold sweat. My partner, Quinn, is also squeaky clean."

"He's in thirty thousand to his bookie, Teddi."

"And next week he'll break even. It's the story of Quinn's life. He bets the ponies during racing season…*legally,* I may add. And does amazingly well at the track. He blows it all during football season when he allows whatever woman he's banging to tell him which team has the prettier uniform. If that's the worst thing you have on Quinn, you're in trouble. As for Teddi's…he runs it honestly—because I'd have his balls on a dinner plate if he didn't and he knows it, no matter how charming he may be."

"I wouldn't want to mess with you, Teddi." Agent Petrocelli looked over at me and grinned. "You would have kicked ass at Quantico."

"Listen to me…my restaurant is clean. Quinn may be a Gallo, but he's not a made man."

"You ever see the lunch crowd there? The dinner crowd? It's fifty percent wise guy."

"They think Quinn and I will go under if they don't eat there. They order the most expensive things on the menu." I saw him smirking and I stopped walking and squared off with him. "You think it's easy to have a successful restaurant in this city? Well, it's not. That place is full of wise guys who are simply being nice to us. It has nothing to do with whether or not we're legitimate."

Agent Petrocelli just kept staring at me. He wouldn't respond, which was making me uncomfortable.

"Look…this is all a misunderstanding. You can't send Di back to England. Do you realize that what you're doing is as bad as what you think my family does? You're taking lives and playing with them. Di and I are just chess pieces to you in some big game to get my family."

I put my hands on my hips. He clenched his jaw and looked over to the left, away from me. Could Agent Petrocelli have a conscience?

"That's not true, Teddi."

"Finally…you're saying something. It *is* true. This is all a misunderstanding."

"I don't know about that."

"How would you feel if someone followed you around just because of who your grandfather was?"

"I know more about that life than you think I do."

"Sure you do."

"My grandfather, Teddi, was a big-time gambler. *Big*. He makes Quinn look like a piker. He'd bet ten grand on the coin toss of the Superbowl."

"My grandfather always picks heads."

"Mine picked tails."

I smiled, despite wanting to hate him.

"My father...he hated that life. When things were good...they were pretty terrific. He lived the high life. Best table at the best steakhouse on Long Island. New Cadillac every year. And when the odds turned on my grandfather—and they always turn—things were bad. My grandfather was always looking over his shoulder. My dad hated that uneasiness. So what did he do? My father became a cop. He was so honest, he never took so much as a free doughnut. He raised me to set my sights on the bureau. Helped I was built like a linebacker with a 4.0 GPA. But I believe in what I do. Or I couldn't do it."

"Well..." I softened slightly. "I suppose that's better than doing it because you're simply a prick."

"Does Angelo Marcello know you talk like that?"

"No. And if he knew I was talking to you..."

"I know. I appreciate you called me. I wouldn't want to do anything to jeopardize your safety."

"Please...it's yours that would be in danger."

"You're a piece of work. I'd say the apple doesn't fall far from the tree."

"What's that supposed to mean?" I snapped.

"Believe it or not, it's a compliment. Your grandfather is one of the last of a dying breed. He's a tough old guy…and principled in his own way. You're pretty tough yourself."

"Maybe." I started to walk again. We walked in silence for a while, falling into a rhythm in our footsteps. Finally, I broke the quiet. "I think I know why you believe Diana has something to do with the family. But that package you saw her deliver to my cousin contained cannoli, Agent Petrocelli—"

"Call me Mark."

"It was cannoli, Mark."

He stopped walking again and turned to face me. "Cannoli?"

"Yes. Pastry. With ricotta. From Quinn's second-cousin's bakery, Tessa's, in Brooklyn. I may even still have the receipt."

His chest moved almost imperceptibly, the beginning of a laugh. A loud belly laugh. Agent Mark Petrocelli, of the perfect biceps and pecs, clutched his stomach and leaned over howling with laughter. I started laughing, too. I couldn't help it.

"Pastry!" he yelled into the wind. Then he started laughing again until tears ran down his face. Suddenly, he grabbed both sides of my face and planted a kiss on the end of my nose. I was stunned. And he looked just as stunned.

"I'm so sorry," he said, his face now flushing crimson. "I don't know what made me do that. Jesus…no…I do. Relief."

"Relief?" I had to crane my neck to look up at him. "So you believe me?"

"Yeah. After a while, as an agent, you become your own lie detector. And you know your chess comment before?"

"Uh-huh."

"Well…don't think that doesn't cross my mind or my

conscience once in a while. I didn't want to think you were somehow…involved in anything more dangerous than wearing stolen Jimmy Choos."

My mouth dropped open.

"Yeah. I know about them."

I turned from him and started walking down the path; again he fell right into step with me.

"So you won't ship Diana away?"

"No, not for giving away cannolis. Though I don't know that getting involved with your cousin Anthony is the smartest move she can make. Isn't he the heir apparent?"

"The what?"

"The heir apparent. There's your grandfather. Then, of the sons-in-law and nephews in the family business, shall we say, the obvious heir is Lou. Vito is lazy. Sonny's just plain— forgive me—stupid. Rocky's also not the sharpest knife in the drawer. Next generation, we have your WB-star brother."

"Please…don't mention that stupid show he's on."

"There're no standouts. Except maybe Tony. I've seen his transcripts from Rutgers. He's no dummy."

"There was Sal."

"Yeah…. I'm sorry for your loss."

"Thanks. Sally was one of my favorite cousins. He was so funny… God, he could do these impersonations from *The Godfather.* Drugs…" I shook my head. "It's like the odds turning. You mess with drugs and sooner or later, they turn on you." I thought of Sal. He always had a roll of Life Savers in his pocket when we were kids, and he always gave me the red ones. I was his little Teddi. Seeing him in his casket after he OD'd was one of the hardest things I'd ever had to face. "Look…" I stopped walking. "I don't think I should be talking to you anymore."

"Why?"

"Agent Petro—"

"Mark."

"Mark. Look, if anyone in my family knew I'd even spoken to you today, they'd have me shot."

"What?" He looked stricken.

"An expression…. I have to go."

I turned to walk away.

"One more thing, Teddi."

"Yeah?" I faced him again.

"Be careful with Robert Wharton."

"Why don't you keep out of my love life?"

"I can't help myself," he said. Then he winked.

I whirled around without saying goodbye and made my way out of Central Park, whose trees were turning crimson. I hailed a cab when I got to the exit. Settling into the warmth of the back seat, I thought of Mark Petrocelli and felt something foreign in the pit of my stomach. Some combination of butterflies and giddiness. Then I reminded myself that my loyalties were to family first. And always.

chapter 10

Diana looked stunning for Sunday family dinner. She wore her hair up in a loose chignon with tendrils falling down, and pearl earrings. Her dress fit her perfectly, as if it were custom-made for her narrow shoulders and slender waist.

"Do you think Tony will like it?" She twirled around.

"He'll go crazy." I smiled. I had never seen Di insecure a day in her life. She sailed through New York, men drooling over her.

"And you, Teddi, look smashing!"

I looked down at my Donna Karan jumpsuit, Prada boots. Courtesy of another "truck." I even put on my favorite watch, a delicate antique with diamonds around the face that had belonged to my late grandma Marcello. It always made Poppy happy to see me wearing her jewelry, and I wanted him in as good a mood as possible when he met Robert.

The phone rang. Michel, the doorman, announced that a Mr. Robert Wharton was waiting in the lobby.

"This is either going to be great, or I'm going to wish I was on a slow boat to Naples," I whispered to Diana as we grabbed our coats and headed to the elevator.

Robert owned a BMW. It was shiny and black, with leather seats, and it seemed like he whisked us out to Brooklyn in a half hour.

On the way, he asked me to teach him an Italian phrase to impress my family with. So I taught him *"Piacere—"* nice and simple "—a pleasure to meet you."

"Now, listen Robert," Diana said as we sped along. "Pace yourself with the food."

"Pace myself," he repeated. "Got it. Anything else?"

Lady Di leaned up between the two front seats. "No, no. You are not paying attention."

"Pace myself. I heard you."

"Yes. And I am sure in that educated little mind of yours you are thinking of food consumption of normal mortals. Ordinary human beings. You must ban that thought from your mind."

"Yes," I said, holding his hand. "You are entering into the pantheons of eating."

"Is there such a thing as…oh, I don't know…*stopping* when you're full?" He laughed.

Diana and I both gasped.

"What did I say?"

"Robert, you silly boy," Diana continued. "I fast on Saturdays. What did you have to eat today?"

"I went for breakfast at a diner near my apartment. Eggs. Bacon. Side of toast. It's Sunday. It's the one day I eat a nice breakfast."

Diana slapped his upper arm. "Fool. Bloody fool."

I looked at Robert. "Eating was a no-no. I should have made that clear. It's going to get ugly."

"God…" he muttered under his breath, "I hope I'm ready."

"Of course you're ready." I patted his hand. "They'll love you." But I glanced back at Lady Di. Our expressions spoke volumes. The Marcellos were going to eat *him* alive.

As we pulled up to the house, the family couldn't have been more obvious. Not only was there a Marcello at every window, but I noticed several Gallos. The two sides had made up from the last feud when one of the old-time Gallo brothers—Quinn's uncle—had supposedly cheated at a high-stakes poker game in the basement of Vito's house. I spotted Quinn's father, his uncle. Oh God! Poor Robert. Poor me!

We climbed the steps of my aunt Gina and uncle Rocky's house. I felt like I was heading to my own execution. Dead woman walking!

Every Sunday my aunts and my mother rotated whose house we had dinner at so that no one had to do all the work more than once every six weeks. However, the competition to host the most elaborate and delicious dinner seemed to escalate each Sunday so that whoever's turn it was spent two weeks prior to it cooking and cleaning. My mother used to scream at me for "living" when I lived at home. Not so much as a speck of dust escaped her eye.

Uncle Rocky opened the door before we were at the top of the stairs.

"Piacere," Robert said, perfectly.

Uncle Rocky looked mildly impressed. *"Piacere.* Come in."

As soon as we walked into the house, we were swarmed

by relatives. Everyone wanted to shake Robert's hand, and Di was able to slip to Tony's side virtually unnoticed. Neither of them, I was sure, was anxious to clue the family in as to their date later. Who needed that kind of pressure?

My father took over the introductions. There would be no way for Robert to keep it all straight. Tony, Tony, Tony, Vito, Rocky, Gina, Angela, Angie, another Tony…I was lucky *I* could remember all their names.

Finally, after all the introductions, my father pulled Robert to the side. "Come on, Bobby, let's go watch the game." Daddy pulled out a cigar and lit it, then offered one in cellophane to Robert. I knew what was going on. The men in my family considered it a right of passage to introduce young men to Cuban cigars when they hit about thirteen. Most every one of my cousins had turned green around the gills and puked up their first one. However, over the years, they acquired a taste for them, or at least could chomp and smoke one without throwing up. They considered any man who couldn't smoke a cigar a "pussy."

Robert put his hands up. "No. I don't smoke. But thank you, Mr. Gallo."

He failed test number one. Oh, Robert…perhaps I should have prepared him even more.

"No problem, Bobby." Another test. All names in my family were somehow given a "y" on the end, or in my case, an "i" with a "y" sound—whether you wanted to be called that or not. They even called Quinn "Quinny." The only exception was the "don" himself, my grandfather. He was Angelo. Though I, and my cousins, as well as his daughters, called him Poppy, so I guess he didn't entirely escape.

"No one's called me Bobby since grade school," Robert said, smiling broadly.

"Something wrong with Bobby?"

"No, no, just kind of funny." This he said to my father, who still went by Frankie. Just like in grade school. Robert was failing miserably. And he was off to the den to be left alone with these vultures until dinnertime.

There was no question I couldn't go into the inner sanctum of the den. It was the kitchen for me. So with a sinking heart, I joined the women around the pot of gravy.

"More oregano, Gina. This tastes flat."

"Maddon', but you're all makin' me crazy. Stand back," Aunt Gina snapped. The kitchen was a hundred degrees. Maybe more.

"Open a window," my mother shouted.

"Where's Diana?" someone else asked.

"Here I am," she sang, coming into the kitchen looking slightly pink-cheeked.

"You sick?" Aunt Carmen held the back of her hand to Diana's head. "Feel her. She's hot."

Aunt Tess put her hand to Di's forehead next. "Yeah. Honey…sit down. Whatsa matter?"

"Nothing." She tried to laugh them off. I knew she was just *lovesick,* but they were already arguing over what remedies she needed.

"Tea with lemon and honey."

"Scotch. A shot of Scotch."

"A brandy. Is it your stomach, hon? If it is, blackberry brandy."

"Is it the curse?"

"Thank God for menopause. No more curse."

"She needs fresh air. Open another window."

"Maybe I better take a shot of brandy. Come to think of it, it is my tummy." Diana smiled weakly, playing up her "illness" for all it was worth. She knew the women in the kitchen almost as well as I did, and she loved them. She also knew that if she didn't accept their advice, they'd hound her all day. It was simpler, in the words of Diana, to smile and nod. Instead, she smiled and drank. Two brandies. I had one, too. I was nervous for poor Robert.

At dinner, which we coordinated with military precision to the half time of the Giants game, the first course was scungilli, and next came the heads. Robert looked pasty. I didn't know whether it was the sight of the heads or if they had talked him into a cigar. He sat beside me, and I squeezed his hand underneath the table.

"So, Robert, what is it you do?" my mother asked politely.

"I'm a television journalist. I'm actually going to be switching over to the *Jerry Turner* show."

"Really?" My mother said the word *really* as if it had three syllables, and a murmur went around the table. The last guy I'd brought home was my high school boyfriend. And he'd said all of three words before he escaped, never to be heard from again. He went off to college and sent me a "Dear Jane" letter.

"Jerry Turner? That *jamook?*" my uncle Vito said derisively.

"Jamook?" Robert asked politely.

"Idiot," I said underneath my breath.

"What?" Robert turned to me.

"Uncle Vito thinks Turner's an idiot. A jerk."

"Acch," Aunt Gina said. "I watch Jerry Turner every night. The man is a god. A *god.*" She said god also as a three-syllable word.

Suddenly a five-minute verbal war broke out over

whether Turner was an ass or not. I looked over at Poppy. He didn't tolerate Sunday disruptions for long.

"Enough," he said. "I say…okay, so he does the show."

I contained a smirk. My grandfather, God love him, was so used to his word being law.

"Oh—" Robert smiled around the table "—I assure you all that I will do only the best shows. I know—" he held up his hands "—he sometimes does some…salacious shows. But I'm after the truth."

"That fuckin' asshole once tried to do a show on Pop," Sonny said.

"Really?" Robert looked pale.

"Yeah. Don't you know who you fuckin' work for?" Sonny asked, then plucked the eyeball from his baby sheep's head, held it on the ends of the tines of his fork, then popped it in his mouth and chewed ever so slowly, trying to intimidate Robert.

"Yeah. Yes. Um…" He looked desperate to change the subject and turned his head to look at my dad. "What do you do, Mr. Gallo?"

Inwardly I cringed. After all, I still didn't know what it was my father did. Or at least what he told Uncle Sam he did.

"Me? I'm a waste-management executive."

"I see."

I looked imploringly at Diana, then Tony. For once, he rescued me instead of torturing me.

"So you think the Giants are going all the way, Bobby?"

"I'm an Eagles fan myself."

"The Eagles? How can you bring dis guy home, Teddi Bear?" Uncle Sonny asked, but an appreciative laugh went around the table, and everyone began arguing about a much safer subject—sports.

Five courses later, Robert looked like he was going to be sick. In fact, if it wasn't so early in our relationship, I think he would have undone the top button of his pants like some of my cousins and uncles, but he didn't.

Tony suddenly stood and stretched. "Aunt Gina? I'll take my dessert to go. I gotta head back to my place."

"What?" his mother asked. This was sacrilege.

"Yeah. Poker game."

"Oh," she said, somewhat approvingly. Poker was an acceptable excuse. It was a man's man game.

Di kicked me under the table.

"We should go, too. Robert has a big day tomorrow, and Diana wasn't feeling too well earlier."

"Sure, kids."

My aunt Gina packed us enough desserts to feed our apartment building, and we went and found our coats. Robert shook everyone's hand again and thanked them for "such a lovely time."

We all got to the door and bid the family a final goodbye. It hadn't gone well. I only hoped he could grow on them, because I knew as soon as we pulled out of the driveway, my uncles' first word would be *mortadella*.

Italian slang for loser.

"I thought that went really well," Robert said in the car, too oblivious to the situation. "Once I smoked one of those awful cigars, they seemed to really accept me."

Sure.

But I didn't care. I squeezed his hand. "I'm sure they liked you."

"I'm taking them all to the Giants game in two weeks."

"What?"

Diana slapped the back of his head.

"Glad you did that, Di. Saved me from doing it."

"What?" Robert looked over at me. "I thought it would be nice. I happen to have tickets. Eight seats in a skybox. I thought your uncles could come, your father and grandfather. Tony."

"Are you trying to end up in a concrete barrel under the end zone?" I asked incredulously.

"What?"

"Jimmy Hoffa. That's where he's rumored to be buried, you know. Meadowlands' end zone."

"You are *kidding* me?"

"No. I'm not. Though Uncle Carmine swears, from a very good source, Hoffa was actually killed in a restaurant and fed through a meat grinder, body piece by body piece."

Robert cringed. "Nice mental picture, thanks."

"I'm just teasing, Robert. But do you really think you're ready to spend time with them alone?"

"I thought it would be a good way to get to know them." He lifted my hand to his lips and kissed it.

Diana snapped, "Well, next time you have a thought like that, suppress it. Bury it. Slap your own bloody head."

"You know," Robert said. "I am beginning to think you two are a little paranoid. Teddi, your family was very nice. They welcomed me. They were lovely. Just like you."

Di spoke up from the back seat. "Please…I am going to vomit. You have abso*bloody*lutely no idea what Uncle Carmine is like when the Giants are losing. I wasn't even *raised* on American football, but I know enough to check how they're doing in the papers before we go out to Sunday dinner."

"Well," Robert laughed, "they usually do terribly."

"Precisely," Diana said, continuing her rant. "Fine. Go watch your little football game. I hope you leave with your ten little fingers to drive home from it."

"I thought I'd get a limo so we could drink. Enjoy ourselves."

I punched him in the shoulder. "Alcohol? Excessive alcohol added to the mix? What is your religious background, Robert?"

"Episcopal. Why?"

"They have a rosary?"

"No."

"Good God, then, invoke whatever the hell the Episcopalians do. But God rest your soul."

As we crossed the bridge back to the city, Diana said, "Tony's meeting us in front of our apartment building. You two want to come out with us? Just going for a quiet drink somewhere."

"No, that's all right. I told you, you go have your special first date with Tony."

"Tony?" Robert asked.

"Yes."

"The big guy?"

"They're all big guys. Except for scrawny Jack. Jackie," Di corrected herself.

Robert smirked. "No offense, but he doesn't seem your type."

"Tall, dark and devastatingly handsome? What's not to like in that type?" Di retorted.

Wonderful. Now he was pissing off my best friend.

"It's not that, but getting entangled with…you know. He's—"

"Careful, Robert. You may not want to finish that sentence," Di warned. Then she switched the conversation. To George Michael. She'd brought along a CD in her purse and begged Robert to put it on his stereo. He complied, and I'll give the man credit. He sang just as loudly as we did all the way home.

What's not to like about a man who's willing to sing to Wham!?

★ ★ ★

Traffic was surprisingly heavy for a Sunday, and it took us fifty-five minutes to get home. Tony was waiting outside our apartment building, leaning up against the hood of his car. Robert found a spot on the street—a miracle in and of itself—and Diana practically leapt from the car and ran across the street to Tony's arms. I didn't want to be a voyeur, but the kiss between them gave *me* goose bumps.

She turned to wave to me, and they took a stroll up the sidewalk, apparently oblivious to the chill that had settled over the city. It smelled like an early first snow might be in the air.

"Do you want to come up?" I asked Robert.

"Sure." He smiled at me. "I had a great time with your family, Teddi. I really liked them. They seemed so...normal."

"*Normal* is not an adjective I usually apply to them. But you've endeared yourself to me for your naiveté."

"I'm not sure what I expected—I suppose maybe Joe Pesci types, you know, sort of ranting. Or the Sopranos or something."

"Give them time. Trust me...they get into trouble—just like the wise guys in the movies. I've spent more than one Christmas with my father needing us to make bail for him."

We got out of his car and went into the building. Until that moment, I hadn't stopped to think about how Diana's relationship with Tony meant I was actually free to do what I wanted. He wouldn't be outside on the street, guarding the "don's" only granddaughter.

When we reached apartment 26A, I unlocked the door and Robert and I stepped inside. I turned on the light and went into the kitchen to fetch us some champagne.

"Make yourself comfortable on the couch," I called out to him. When I came out to join him, he had turned on the stereo to a jazz station and was waiting for me, his arm draped along the back of the couch. I sat down and noticed how perfectly I fit in the crook of his arm.

I handed him the bottle. "Care to do the honors?"

He uncorked the bottle and poured us each a glass. He raised his in a toast. "To the most beautiful Teddi Bear in the world." We clinked and sipped. Then he leaned over and kissed me, gently at first, then more urgently.

I kissed him back, biting him softly on the lower lip until I heard him moan.

"You're making me crazy," he breathed.

We kissed for what seemed like a half hour. I had to be honest with him.

"I can't ask you to spend the night, Robert."

"Why? Diana? She'll be out until late."

"No." I moved away from him a little bit. "Because given my life, given my family, I've not been close to too many people. I just need time. I have to feel completely comfortable. Completely trust you."

"You don't trust me?" He seemed hurt.

"I do. I just need to get to know you a little better."

He cupped my face in his hands. "It's your call."

"I know. And you are so terribly sweet."

He kissed me again, and then, fifteen minutes later, he kissed my cheek. "If I'm going to stop this, I need to do it now." He smiled at me. "You're making me completely nuts. Besides, I have an early call tomorrow. See you later in the week?"

I nodded. We both stood, and I walked him to the door. With one final, very passionate kiss, we said good-night. I opened the door, then shut it behind him.

I walked back through my apartment and to my bed-room, stripping out of my jumpsuit, which was admittedly a little askew. Robert had unbuttoned the top two buttons and had played with the little bow on my bra. I felt a touch of regret. Should I have slept with him? Yes, it was early on, but he had already been willing to meet my family. What did that say about the man?

I brushed my teeth and flicked on my television, search-ing for *Law & Order*. I found an episode and climbed into bed. Instead of regrets and thoughts of Robert, I thought of Mark Petrocelli. I wasn't sure why. He just had this awful habit of drifting into my thoughts.

I thought of the reason I had given Robert for not let-ting him stay—that I needed to trust him fully. Maybe the person I didn't quite trust was myself.

Late that night, Di opened the door to my room.

"Teddi? You awake?"

I'd only been dozing. I think part of my subconscious was waiting to see what time she came home.

"Sort of."

"Number one."

"What?" The television was still on. She glowed in the light of, now, images of a rerun of *Cheers* being broadcast.

"He's officially moved to the spot of number-one kisser ever in the life of Diana Kent."

"Holy crap!" I sat up, pulling the covers around me, still a little groggy. "That's saying an awful lot."

"I know. You do know I had a crush on Prince Andrew while growing up, and though I've never kissed Prince An-drew, I have imagined it, and I have since decided kissing him would be like kissing a bowl of pudding."

"Pudding?"

"Mushy."

"*Musciata,* in Italian."

"Yeah. That. But kissing Tony is in another category altogether. He's so…strong yet not too strong. He grabbed my hair."

"I love that." I now noticed her hair was no longer in a chignon but was loose and around her shoulders, a rich honey-blond.

"I would have slept with him, but he was so gentlemanly, he didn't even ask."

"Madonna-whore."

"What? What about Madonna? And yes, she is a little whorish."

"Yes. But I didn't mean *that* Madonna. I meant Madonna-whore. Italian men are known for seeing their loves as rather virginal and their lovers as whores. Their *goomahs.*"

"So what does that mean exactly."

"It means he thinks of you in the highest regard. That you're not some *puttana* to him. You're special. He loves you. Or he's falling in love with you."

"If he's expecting me to be a virgin—"

"He's not that stupid."

"Thanks a lot."

"No. I just mean he respects you."

"Well, all I can say is when we finally do sleep together, it will be unbelievable."

"I'm sure."

"And how did it go with Robert?"

"Really well."

"What's wrong?"

"Nothing."

Lady Di shook her head. "I can tell when something's wrong."

"Well..." I sighed. "I didn't think it went all that great with the family. He's so well mannered and frankly, I don't think he fully understands the whole family thing. The Marcellos and the Gallos...well, we don't have to go there for the thousandth time."

"Your family will get used to him, Teddi. Even Tony said all they care is that you're happy."

"I don't know.... Robert is so unbelievably sweet. Thoughtful. He even has adapted to the fact that I'm in the restaurant business, which means weird hours, erratic schedule. Remember Alex?"

"The one who got in that argument with Quinn?"

I nodded. Alex was a nine-to-five computer programmer I met through one of the waitresses—before the waitress quit because she was in love with Quinn and he was in love with someone else that week. Alex had come on really strong and had taken to hanging out on a bar stool every night waiting for me to get off work. "Yeah, Di. I mean, it's not every guy who can adapt to restaurant hours. Robert works strange and long hours, too. It kind of works."

"Well, what else is bothering you?" She grabbed my hand. "All I have is my stuck-up brother and his stick-in-the-ass wife. You, darling, are my true-blue sister, though God only knows how he brought the two of us together. What was Boston University thinking when they roomed us together? Two opposites. One all over the shop, just a total mess, the other neat as a pin. One who has taken a vow of—what the hell is it called?"

"What?"

"That vow of silence thing?"

"An *omerta*. What happens in the family stays in the family."

"Yeah. That. The other…well, my family is oh-so-stiff. I am telling you my father could die and they could stuff the corpse at the dinner table and we wouldn't even notice. Staple his eyelids shut, we'd never know."

"That's gruesome."

"Sorry. I watched *Six Feet Under* last week."

"But we ended up the best of friends, Di."

"As you would say, 'Go figure.'"

"Go figure."

"So tell your dear chum, Lady Di, what else is troubling you?"

"Agent Petrocelli."

"He's your James Bond. You can be his Octopussy."

"Di!"

She was still holding my hand, and she squeezed it.

"I don't know why," I suddenly blurted out, "but he…I don't know. Maybe it's that he's from another world. You know…the good guys. The supposed good guys. Maybe it's some stupid fascination."

"Maybe it's just kismet."

"Maybe. But really…it's impossible. Maybe that's what hurts a tiny bit."

We were silent a moment. She leaned over and kissed my cheek. "I'm off to bed, dear, darling Teddi. But you know, like Tony and me. If it's meant to be…"

"Don't even go there." I scrunched down under the covers. "Good night, Di."

"Good night."

I willed myself to think of Robert Wharton. That's all I wanted. Someone ordinary. Someone who hadn't taken an *omerta*, but who also didn't wear a badge. Was that so much to ask?

chapter 12

Office Memorandum: United States Government
TO: David Cameron
FROM: Mark Petrocelli, Special Agent in
Charge, Federal Bureau of Investigation
SUBJECT: Wiretap report, Angelo Marcello,
Marcello's Restaurant, Brooklyn, New York

6:20 p.m.

Angelo Marcello: Diana…thank you for com-
ing to this emergency family meeting.
Diana Kent: Hello, Grandpa Angelo—
Angelo Marcello: Call me Poppy. I think of
you as my other granddaughter.
Diana Kent: Thank you, Poppy.
Angelo Marcello: Do you think of me as a
tired old man, Diana?

Diana Kent: No. Not much escapes you, does it?

Angelo Marcello: Not much at all. Like I know about you and Tony. And I approve.

Diana Kent: Thank you. That means the world to me. Sneaky devils you all are…figuring that out all on your own.

Angelo Marcello: Diana…I noticed you and Tony before you and Tony noticed each other. You were struck by the thunderbolt.

Diana Kent: Oh, dear…I heard that's not a good thing.

Angelo Marcello: Eh…you don't listen to Teddi. She just thinks of my wife's younger brother Mario. The thunderbolt is a good thing. I was struck when I saw my wife—of course she was just fourteen and I was sixteen, but I knew. We were married fifty years. Fifty years. Not many people can say that…. You know, not one Marcello has ever been divorced. We don't do that. We stick it out. And even so…fifty years is impressive, isn't it?

Diana Kent: It is. I remember the anniversary party. In fact, I think…yes, you all taught me how to play craps that night. I lost.

Angelo Marcello: Yeah, but I made Vito give you your money back.

Diana Kent: Quite right. Very good of you.

Angelo Marcello: So the way I see it, you

and Tony...it's a good thing. Now, we have to talk about Teddi...

Sonny Santucci (Angelo Marcello's son-in-law): You understand that we're all here because we care about Teddi.

Frank Gallo: Trust me, Diana, when the Gallos sit down with the Marcellos, it must be serious.

Diana Kent: Well...now you're all making me a touch nervous. Do you suppose I could have a glass of red wine?

Vito Marucci (Angelo Marcello's son-in-law): Pour Diana a glass of wine.

Diana Kent: Thank you.

Carmine Agnelli: Diana, you know that Connie and I love Teddi like a daughter, but this guy—

Frank Gallo: Guy. Bullshit. He's a slimeball. A *worm*. And he needs to be squashed.

Diana Kent: I take it you're referring to Robert.

Angelo Marcello: Teddi's father here is a little excitable. Allow me to explain. We don't think this Robert is the right person for Teddi.

Diana Kent: But it's very early in the relationship. I don't think you have anything to worry about. Besides, Teddi is a very bright girl. Isn't it for her to decide?

Angelo Marcello: You know, Diana, Teddi is the first woman in the family to have a business. She works hard, and we're all very

proud of her, but we also assumed one day
she would settle down, get married, raise
a family. That's the Marcello way, the Gallo
way. We believe in family.

Diana Kent: But girls today...she has time.
Truly, I wouldn't get all worried just yet.

Angelo Marcello: As a family, we don't want
to see her get hurt. This man...he's no good.
We've done some checking. *Si capisce che*...he
is no good.

Diana Kent: I get you. Um...*capiche.*

Angelo Marcello: We think he's what we say
in this family, a *strunz.*

Diana Kent: I take it that's not a good
thing.

Frank Gallo: You got that fuckin' right.

Angelo Marcello: Please, Frank, there's a
lady present.

Diana Kent: Is there a reason, other than
perhaps he's a little stiff? You know, in
that way, he's a little British.

Frank Gallo: We got our reasons.

Angelo Marcello: Anyway, Diana...all we ask
is that you watch out for Teddi's best interests, too. And perhaps you don't encourage her in this little love affair. The less
encouragement she receives, the better.

Diana Kent: Well...there is someone else she
likes. In that thunderbolt way, I think,
only she won't admit it, of course.

Vito Marucci Jr. (Angelo Marcello's grandson): Who?

Diana Kent: Well...let me just keep that to myself. I've taken a little *omerta*. See, I am catching on. I even know what that means. But you just leave this all to me.

Angelo Marcello: If you can get her away from this boy, the family would owe you a debt of gratitude.

Diana Kent: Poppy, I love Teddi as much as you all.

Angelo Marcello: We know. You're a good girl, Diana. How about some dinner?

Diana Kent: I'm starved. I'm telling you, if I had been born Italian, I would weigh two hundred and fifty pounds.

chapter 13

Robert sent me a dozen roses at work on Wednesday of that week. A dozen red, long stemmed, in a handblown crystal vase. I called to thank him. I could only remember one other time that I was sent flowers, and those were make-up flowers after a big fight, not "I-just-think-you're-beautiful flowers."

"Thank you, Robert, they're gorgeous."

"Not half as beautiful as you."

"Okay…now you're going completely over the top." I laughed.

"Can't a man send his girlfriend flowers?"

I was silent.

"Um…the woman he's dating," he corrected. "I don't mean to scare you off."

"That's all right. Really. And they're lovely."

"Can I come to Teddi's for lunch today?"

"I'd love it. The special is a veal Florentine. I highly recommend it."

"I'll drop by at noon. And I'll have the special."

"See you then."

After I hung up with Robert, I speed-dialed Diana.

"Diana Kent," she sang into the phone.

"Guess who just sent me a dozen long-stemmed roses?"

"James Bond."

"No."

"Oh, damn." She sounded crestfallen. "No *Live and Let Die*? No *Octopussy*? No *From Russia with Love*?"

"No. They're with love all right, but from Robert. For no reason. Just because he cares—and thinks I'm beautiful. What do you think?"

"I think…um…"

"What?"

"I think that maybe you're right. I think that your family and Robert…well…how can it ever work?"

"Diana, you said it yourself. They can't very well expect me to date a mobster. They'll get used to him."

"I don't know, Teddi. This is a lot to get used to. You're from two different worlds. Didn't you say his family is old money? Snobbish money. Can you imagine him saying to Mumsy, 'Why, Mumsy, we're off on a foxhunt. And may I mention…I'm dating the granddaughter of Angelo Marcello'?"

"You're from old money. Old British money. Your parents love me."

"Pish posh. They don't so much love you as hate me. They love you to spite me. I could live with…with, oh, I don't know, a serial killer and they'd think it was fine so long as I wasn't living with *them*."

"Thanks."

"Nothing personal. I just hope you know what you're getting into."

"I thought you understood. I thought you liked Robert."

"Well, that was before he was so serious as to send you a dozen red roses."

"It's not serious. It's a very nice gesture, though, don't you think?" Diana was suddenly acting quite strange.

"Yes. What am I saying? Of course!"

"Thanks. I thought so, too. He's coming here for lunch."

"Lunch? Splendid… And what about our FBI agent?"

"*Our* agent? He's not our agent. He's the enemy, Diana. Don't forget that."

"Well, it's easy to forget that when you're looking at biceps that are like…well, like big massive hunky biceps."

"Articulate."

"Thank you."

"Is Tony telling you he doesn't like Robert, Diana? Is he turning you against this whole thing?"

"Tony would do nothing of the sort. He's said a dozen times he just wants you to be happy." She sounded very hurt.

"I'm sorry. I didn't mean to accuse Tony of anything. Listen, I've got to go. I'm really happy, Diana. Tell me you're happy for me."

"Delirious."

"Thanks. Love ya."

"Love you, too. Hugs and kisses, x's and o's."

I hung up the phone. Diana sounded…disapproving. Melancholy. It was Tony, I was sure of it. Maybe her dating one of the Marcello clan wasn't that good an idea after all.

Two hours later, I stood over Robert's table in my chef coat and checked pants, a red handkerchief around my neck, my hair up in a bun, and waited for his veal verdict.

"This is perfect. Unbelievable. Now you're in big trouble. I'm going to ask you to cook for me at home." He winked at me and spontaneously reached out his hand to hold mine.

Being a chef is not particularly glamorous. Your skin is constantly exposed to oil and steam, your coat to splatters and stains. Your hair has to be pulled up and in a hairnet or a hat or kerchief. In short, it is not for the cosmetically insecure. For instance, Diana, who I think was *born* wearing lipstick, would sooner break some legs for my uncle Vito than work in a restaurant. Yet Robert seemed oblivious to my less-than-sexy appearance.

"Isn't that your uncle Lou and cousin Tony?"

"Where?" I feigned ignorance, craning my neck.

"Over there. In the corner."

"So it is. I told you my family comes in a lot."

"I should ask them to join me. It would be the polite thing to do."

Politeness. In my family, there was no such thing as politeness. Everything was everybody's business. After Sunday dinner, my mother had phoned to say she was quite "taken" with my "beau" because he was on the *Jerry Turner* show. My father, she said (he wouldn't use up his twelve-word monthly allotment), thought Robert was "a little wormy." I just rolled my eyes. I consider rolled eyes the Italian version of Diana's "smile and nod."

"They're almost done, Robert. They don't linger over lunch."

"Well then, I'll ask them over to my table for some dessert and coffee. You can't tell me they pass up homemade tiramisu."

Actually, *nothing* came between Uncle Lou and his dessert. But just as he was about to invite them over, Quinn came and sat down in the chair opposite Robert and stuck out his hand. Robert let go of my hand and reached over to shake Quinn's.

"Teddi's favorite cousin and partner, Quinn."

"Robert Wharton. Nice to meet you."

"Funny, you don't look insane."

"I beg your pardon?"

"Dating Don Angelo Marcello's *only* granddaughter? Are you crazy, man? The Gallo side is bad enough."

I slammed my foot into Quinn's instep. "*Thanks* so much for dropping by, Quinn, but I think there's an *emergency* in the kitchen."

"Ow! That's your territory. So, Robert, can I get you a bit of sambuca?"

"No. I'd fall asleep this afternoon, and I have a big interview with an assistant D.A."

"You know what D.A. stands for in this family, right?" Quinn asked.

"District attorney?"

Quinn shook his head. "Dumb ass."

Robert laughed and wiped his mouth with a linen napkin. "I was going to stay for dessert, but I should really go."

"Lunch is on me," Quinn said.

"I couldn't let you do that. I didn't expect that."

"Don't worry about it. Just tip the waitress pretty good. Cammie is mad at me."

I glared at Quinn.

He shrugged. "Sorry, little cuz, she accused me of flirting with a Central Park Wester last night. Now, other faults aside, Teddi honey, baby, you *know* the trust-fund set is not my type. They, on the other hand, are irresistibly drawn to the bad boy. But they're worse than Main Line Philly. So boring." He affected a yawn.

I shook my head in exasperation. "Robert's from Philly."

"Oh. Sorry there, Robert. But then again, I can call it like it is because *I'm* not dating you."

Robert didn't look the slightest bit irritated. Like everyone, he accepted Quinn's motormouth because Quinn said everything as if it were an intimate joke between best friends.

"Good thing we're not dating, Quinn. I'm sure the family would have an even harder time accepting that."

"Good one, Robert. And you're right. We kind of wondered for a while if Michael, Teddi's brother, might be gay. He was always primping in the mirror, had this whole 'I'm-so-beautiful' thing going."

I shook my head. The original mirror freak was talking about *my brother* and the mirror? I looked at Robert. "My brother loves blondes with lots of silicone, so this wondering didn't go on for long."

Robert smiled.

Quinn continued, "True enough. So, Robert…I hear you met the family on Sunday."

"Yeah. It went pretty well."

"Hmm. Did you find a dead fish in your car after it was over?"

"No."

"No one left a dead rat on your welcome mat?"

"No."

"I suppose that's a start, then. Hey…what are you?"

Robert looked completely confused.

"Italian…Irish…what?"

"White Anglo-Saxon Protestant, my friend."

Quinn made the sign of the cross. "Buddy, if you can put up with the Gallos and Marcellos for my cousin here, you must be an all-right guy." Then he stood up, said goodbye and walked over to the bar.

I sat down where Quinn had been. "Well, that's the opinionated, bigmouthed, arrogant yet adorable Quinn. I've got to get back to the kitchen. Chef Jeff will likely poison our customers."

"And you left him in charge of your kitchen?"

"Not for long." I shook my head, smiling. "He's just a kid. Nineteen. Wants to learn to cook more than anything. Unless you count body 'design.' Spends a portion of *every* paycheck on either a piercing or a tattoo. Don't think there's *anything* not pierced. Including you-know-where. Tribal tattoos everywhere. Good cook but can't remember directions well. So if I say, 'Put in two teaspoons of oregano,' and then I'm off doing something else, he'll forget, won't ask and add two heaping *tablespoons.* This is okay when we're dealing with oregano. This was not okay when he added two cups of salt to the gravy instead of a few dashes of sugar. Anyway, he has no family. Lives in a shithole apartment. And Quinn and I are fond of him."

Robert just stared at me.

"What?"

"Every time I think you can't be more perfect, you tell me something like this."

"What, that I hire incorrigible punks with nose and penis piercings?"

"No. That you give someone a chance."

I shrugged. "Trust me...I'm no saint."

I stood and then leaned down to kiss him. From across the restaurant, I could see Tony and Uncle Lou's obvious displeasure at a public display of affection. I ignored them and went back to the kitchen. Chef Jeff had a small disaster on his hands…carmelized onions that had gone from carmelized straight through to burned beyond recognition.

"Don't worry, Jeff…just start a new pan of them."

"Okay. Hey, Teddi…have to show you my calf. Have a new tattoo. Green-and-red dragon."

"Delightful."

After the lunch crowd dispersed, Quinn came back and signaled me to come to the bar.

"What's up?"

"Have a seat, cuz." He poured me a sambuca, and then he poured himself one.

"What?"

"Pip just called."

Pip was our name—Quinn's and Lady Di's actually—for our accountant. Pip, as in Pipsqueak. Roger Peterson was five foot two in stockinged feet with a tiny build and delicate bone structure that made him look like a real live elf.

"And?"

"And we're going to have trouble making payroll this month."

"We've been slammed…busy. How could we be running in the red?"

"We're not turning tables on Friday night the way we should. We're not getting the late-night crowd. We're getting family…but they linger. And without them, we're not filling the place. Now, I know you don't want to meet Di's—"

"Don't even say it." He was referring to Lady Di's scheme to have me write a Mafia cookbook and meet with a literary agent she knew.

"You need to think about it. Discuss it with Di."

"Quinn, if I tell you something, and swear you to secrecy, will you keep the *omerta?*"

Quinn was leaning on the bar, staring straight at me as I sat in a stool. "Look," he said, "*I* was the one who found a severed hand in your grandfather's extra freezer. You're the only one I ever told that to."

"Good. Then we're clear...." I downed the rest of my sambuca in a shot.

"Does this have something to do with loverboy? Are you—" he lowered his voice "—pregnant?"

I shoved at him over the bar. "No, I'm not pregnant, you idiot!"

"What, then?"

"The FBI is snooping around."

"What?" He looked around the place. Everyone in my family could spot a cop or a fed inside of thirty seconds, from their shoes to their haircuts, to their posture. We were raised to know the good guys—us—from the assholes—them.

"He's not here. This one agent in particular. Family shit. You know how it goes. I think he believes we're legit, but face it, we both have family on the wrong side of the legal system, and we own the *classic* money-laundering business. If we were selling pizza pies, we'd be in hand-cuffs, I swear."

"Pip makes sure every number adds up."

"Thanks to *me*. You'd cook the books if you could. No...it's not like they could find anything, anyway. Not here."

"And what does that have to do with Di's idea of making this place the hottest joint in town? She's offered to do some PR...if you do a cookbook...."

"It's just *not* a good time to draw attention to ourselves."

"I'm still for it."

I was silent. I pushed my glass forward. "Pour me another sambuca."

"Sure thing." He filled my small brandy snifter and added three more coffee beans. "We need extra luck and prosperity."

"You know why we are a good pair, Quinn?"

"You can cook, and I can bring the crowds in….and charm them. Let's not forget charm them."

"Yeah, that. And you're a detail man. You can spot a wineglass with water spots from ten tables away. But also I do the big-picture thinking, and you can't think past the end of your penis."

"I beg your pardon?"

He stood upright from where he was leaning on the bar, and I could see his perfectly cut physique shown off to perfection in his black silky T-shirt. "I don't do all my thinking with my dick, Teddi."

"Yes. You do." I said it softly. A little sadly. "Even the ponies. You don't think I've figured out the reason you love them is the rush, the orgasm, when you win, when your filly is turning the last lap and you're urging her on."

"I run the front of the house…I have it spinning like a top. That's not fair to characterize me that way." He looked genuinely insulted, but he also didn't look me in the eye. Because he knew I was right.

"Yes. You do a great job running the front of the house. But have you noticed our help can be categorized in two ways…? In the kitchen we have Leon, with a shaved head, hip-hop clothes and a nose that has *clearly* been broken more than five times. He can barely breathe through it. He has to wear those breathing strips across it so he can get air when it's hot and we're busy. Then we have Chef

Jeff, he of the tribal tattoos and pockmarked skin but heart of gold. We have Luis, who comes in to do prep work and is missing three fingers on his right hand, as well as an eye. He makes vague references to incarceration and is entirely too handy with knives. And we have Ju–Ju–B, whose real name we don't even know, who works with Leon and is just plain homely and claims to worship the devil."

"And your point?"

"Then we have the front of the house. There are models who don't have the looks our girls have."

"What? You want me to," he whispered, "hire girls with missing eyeballs?"

"Quinn, our bartender is so magnificent, she has modeling agents pass her their cards weekly."

"I still don't get why Tatiana won't at least go *meet* with these guys. They're from legit places. She could be making a lot of money."

"Are you that dumb?"

"What?" Quinn looked at me, his blue eyes absolutely void of cognition.

"She stays because she loves you. She will do anything to be near you. She is a masochist who, unlike the others, hasn't quit over you."

Quinn's eyes looked shiny. "What?" he asked hoarsely. Tatiana was nearly six feet tall, with blue eyes and black hair. If she and Quinn ever made a baby, it would be beautiful.

"Look Quinn…the point I'm making is that you think with your testosterone, and I think with a plan. This crackpot idea of Diana's and yours isn't a good 'big picture' idea. I can't do a 'Mafia' cookbook. Not with the FBI parked in a van up the block."

I finished my second sambuca. "Leon is in back. I'm going home. Tell the girls to push desserts and check averages up. Push the specials. We'll make payroll. We always do."

With that I trudged out the door and headed home. I was tired. Of everything.

Later that night, I cooked a simple meal for Diana and myself, relaxing, barefoot in my own kitchen. We usually do takeout, as on my nights off I don't necessarily like to cook, but I needed to lose myself in the process. In rubbing the garlic and chopping the parsley. In the scents and ritual of cooking a meal. I felt myself relax. It was like being taken back to grandma's kitchen with a towel tied around my waist and the approving pats on the head from my grandmother as she showed me how to coax the garlic from its skin.

As soon as Diana walked through the door, she smelled dinner simmering.

"Oh, God, I am famished! I love you, Teddi. Love you, love you, love you! Let me go change."

"Okay. I opened a bottle of red. It's breathing."

"Not for long! We'll *kill* it."

Diana went back to her bedroom and changed into her version of "casual clothes"—a stunning pair of silk lounging pajamas.

"How was the lunch crowd?" she asked, twisting her hair up into a loose chignon and setting plates on our dining room table. We had a set of beautiful antique china she inherited from her grandmother. In fact, we had enough to feed forty. But it mostly sat in a china hutch. We were too busy to eat properly…and we always had Teddi's and a dozen Chinese places to feed us.

"Well…" I called from the kitchen. "Robert came in and tried the special. Saw the place. Loved it."

"Good," she said without much enthusiasm.

"Is something wrong, Di? You were so fired up to have me in the hay with Robert, and now you seem a lot less enthused."

"Oh, no…it's nothing. Really. Go on."

I padded out and put the pasta on the table, brought out the salad, poured us both a glass of wine and sat down.

"Anyway, he seemed just as captivated by my appearance in my chef's coat as in Donna Karan."

"I find that odd, but in a good way. You know, I once dated a man who liked me to dress like a schoolmarm. Buttoned up. Prim and proper. Totally unsexy. But it rocked his universe."

"Bet you ended that quick."

"You got that right. I think he kept hoping I'd spank him on the bottom in the bedroom. Not for me." She shook her head. "You naughty, naughty boy. Bend over for the headmistress!" She laughed and pushed a stray tendril behind her ear.

"Di, have you been talking to Quinn again about that idea of yours?"

"The cookbook?"

"Uh-huh."

"Not lately, though I still think it would be marvelous. I know it sounds a little…exploitative…but face it, Americans love all things mob. It's terribly…well, American. Ever see the movie *The Krays*?"

I shook my head.

"'Bout a British gang. We find mobsters unsightly. Frightening. Ghastly. The movie was stylized, but they had all these sick mommy issues. You Americans find mobsters glamorous."

"Not me personally."

"No. Not you personally, but your culture. The Brits want to lock them up and throw away the keys. Americans want their mob men eating Italian food in restaurants. I think if you did it, you'd get a good bit of publicity—with Kent PR handling it all gratis, of course. I owe it to you for all the free meals you and Quinn have given me."

I nodded. "I know you're right—about how Americans embrace the mob—but I don't get it. I mean, aside from Sundays...the food and the boisterousness...all wonderful...why care about a bunch of men who have made their living off of bookmaking, loansharking and all the rest of it? Why care who's a made man, who's the don?"

"It's that *Godparent* movie."

"*Godfather.*"

"Yes. *Godfather.* The one where they put a dog's head in bed with that man."

"It was a horse's head."

"Yes. That one. Did I ever tell you I would do the young Al Pacino in a heartbeat? I bet he's not all mouth and no trousers, that's for sure."

"Yes. In fact, you also said you would do the young De Niro."

"I did? Hmm." She lifted her fork, poised in the air. "Let me think about it just a moment... Why, yes I would."

"You always love the Italian movie stars. You were destined for Tony, I can see that now. *The Godfather* started it. But you've gotten much worse. Now you even like the guy who plays Tony Soprano."

"In a big-bear-ravish-me sort of way."

"I still don't get it."

"Ever do a search of *Marcello* on the Internet?"

"No. I'm lucky I have time to pee at work, let alone get on the computer to do a search."

"An ungodly, ghastly number of sites come up. Hundreds of thousands. And people have fan clubs. Did you know there are even Internet serial killer sites?"

"Charming."

She twirled her spaghetti. "Look, all I am saying is that I recently met with Anna Friedman, a literary agent, and when I *happened* to mention over much too much wine who my flatmate was and why I couldn't ever possibly meet her for dinner on Sunday—that it was akin to sacrilege—she had this idea of a Mafia cookbook. Then I thought of the restaurant. Making it a real A-list place. Why not? You never capitalize on the fact that at any given time, if you walk into Teddi's, you will see a real live, honest-to-God *mobster* sitting there eating. For some people, that would be a tourist attraction!"

I cringed a little. "So not my style."

"But the cookbook…listen to me…they have made books, cookbooks, based on *The Sopranos*. Carmela Soprano is not a *real* person. Perhaps they *think* of her as real, thanks to America's obsession with its idiot box, and I do mean idiot, but she is not. You, on the other hand are real. And all the Marcello recipes are real. As are the Gallo recipes. Your mother is real. Aunt Gina is real. Aunt Rose is real. Uncle Rocky is real. Uncle Lou is real. Can you not just see it now? 'Uncle Lou's Spaghetti Carbonara.'"

I nodded. "He actually likes Bolognese."

"You know what I mean."

"I do. I just don't know with James Bond on my tail if that's such a good idea to attract extra attention. But Quinn…he's all for it."

"Of course. He fancies himself an impresario. He fancies opening a Teddi's in Union Square and one in Tribeca. He fancies being so famous that every woman in the world will simply stop dead in her tracks and spread her legs for him, already wet and waiting."

"Di!"

"Well, it is Quinn's ultimate fantasy—although he didn't actually say *that*. And though his reasoning is all wrong, I think you should consider it. Write down your recipes. Start thinking of little stories you can tell along with them…how the recipes were handed down through the Marcello and Gallo generations, from Sicily and Italy to America."

"I guess it wouldn't hurt to write a few things down. Pip *is* being a little bleak in his financial predictions."

"Trust me. You do a cookbook, and you let me have free reign doing PR, and you, my dear, will give Wolfgang Puck a run for his money."

I laughed.

"You think I'm bloody kidding? This pasta is orgasmic!"

I just shook my head. Lady Di and her harebrained schemes. But I had to admit, even to myself, that my pasta kicked ass.

chapter 14

The next night, late, the phone rang. I was watching a *Law & Order* rerun, feeling very achy from a long day on my feet in the restaurant, working a double, and I assumed the caller was Robert.

"Hello, sexy," I said into the telephone.

"Well, hello sexy yourself." The voice was unfamiliar.

"Who is this?"

"Agent Petrocelli...Mark."

I bolted upright. "It's—" I looked at my illuminated clock radio "—twelve-forty-five. What the hell are you doing a) calling and b) calling so goddamn late? What couldn't have waited until the morning?"

"Actually...I saw your light on."

"Pervert or voyeur? Which is it? Or is it both?"

"Neither. I was worried about you."

"Why?"

"First, because of what we spoke about last week."

"I'm fine. As I've already explained to you, I really have nothing to do with any of the family business. And Quinn, other than being a bit of a racetrack junkie, is also straight as an arrow."

"Except when it comes to waitresses."

"What's that supposed to mean?"

"Nothing."

Suddenly, I remembered an exceedingly incompetent waitress who took a little too much interest in Pip the accountant when he came in for lunch. She, after all, was one of Quinn's statuesque beauties, and usually no one wanted to wait on Pip, who was known for being just as anal-retentive about his meals as he was about his ledgers, accounts and Quicken files. He would send his food back three times. Always three, never two, never four. Too much pepper, too little salt, not enough oregano, too much oregano. We always sent back the exact same plate of pasta, slightly reheated in the microwave. On the third attempt, he would suddenly rave. Yet this waitress…Julie, I think her name was…just fawned over him. Over an elf. And it wasn't that he was a big tipper, either. He left precisely, to the penny, fifteen percent.

"Did you by any chance have an agent working undercover at my restaurant? We fired her about four months ago?"

"Why do you ask?"

"Why do you know Quinn has a problem keeping his dick in his pants?"

"Word gets around."

"You know," I said, gathering my comforter around me, "this is why I hate cops. They can't give you a straight answer. It doesn't matter. Snoop all you want. Nothing to find. Good night, Agent Petro—"

"Wait! I said that was the first reason."

"Second?"

"I still need to get Diana the money for her broken shoe."

"Put a check in an envelope. Seal it. Buy a stamp. Put it in a mailbox."

"And…look…most important, I don't know if you're aware, being as I believe you when you say that you don't know much about the family business, but word is the Jersey Corelli family is going to make a move on some of your uncle Sonny's turf."

I shivered slightly. "No…I hadn't heard. My uncles and father and Poppy don't tell me anything. Or my mother and aunts, for that matter. And Quinn, he's so busy with the restaurant—and our waitresses as you point out—that the family considers him a citizen now. They don't keep him in the loop unless it's about getting together to go to the track."

"Listen…this is totally out of line as far as me being an agent goes. But I told myself all night that I wasn't telling you anything your family doesn't already know. The Corelli thing is common knowledge."

"We've been through stuff like this before. Poppy was shot back when I was five. I don't even really remember it."

"I know. But the thing is, your grandfather is getting really old, and these young turks up and coming…they don't give a shit about how things are done. Everybody's looking out for himself, looking for a shortcut. Your uncle Lou is really pissed about things. You need to be careful."

I smiled at his concern. "They're all big boys and know what they're doing. I'm worried, but—you know, it just occurred to me that I don't even know if you're married and have a family."

"What?" he asked, even as I prayed he would say there

was no Mrs. Petrocelli. "No. But what does that have to do with a war brewing between the families?"

"Well, I was going to say that if wives of cops and FBI agents worried each time their husband did something dangerous, they'd go insane. Sometimes, you just have to let it go."

"I never thought of it that way before."

"I love my father with his old Brooklyn ways and his cigars and his pack of cigarettes rolled up in the sleeve of his shirt like it's 1952. I love him. But I've always known, or at least as long as I can remember, that there's another side to this life. It's not all Sunday dinners. Some of it is ugly. But I have to trust them to be careful." I said the words with a wisdom and bravery I didn't feel. The head of the Corelli family was a known hothead with a lot of ambition.

"But Teddi…they all eat in your restaurant. What if the Corellis try something there? I saw Chris Corelli drive past your place five times last week, just circling the block."

"Did Tony and Uncle Lou see him?"

"Yeah."

"That must be why they're eating there twice a day now."

"Please promise me you'll be careful. Extra careful."

"I'll be careful. Look, I think it's totally weird that you've called me at one in the morning. But it's really sweet of you to worry. Thanks for the warning."

There was silence on the other end of the phone.

"Was that all?" I asked.

"Yeah. No…. Listen, with this thing going down, I just want you to know that sometimes we really *are* the good guys. Now, some of the Corellis are real scumbags, pardon my French, but I have to give your family credit. They run a clean operation. No drugs. I don't want to see some of the old guys pass away and watch the crazy Russian mob take over, or the Colombians…or whoever. Most of all, I don't want to see anyone who loves their family as much as your grandfather loves his get hurt. The feds, whatever you think of us, sometimes we really do want to help people, make the world better. All that."

"Very Dudley Do-Right of you."

"Well, let me put it this way. Cops aren't all bad. If you came home and your apartment had been robbed, who would you call? Uncle Lou or 911?"

"I'd choose 911. I'd file a useless police report because there isn't a snowball's chance in hell the police will find a robber in a city this size. Nor do they care when there are rapists and murderers out there. But I would do it because it's what people do. Like one person says 'How are you?' and another says 'Fine' even when they're not fine. *After* I called 911 I would *also* call Uncle Lou so that he could get the word out that if anyone even *thinks* of breaking into my apartment again, they better be prepared to lose their balls. Literally. Then Uncle Lou would help me replace my stolen everything because the insurance company would give me the runaround. Because that business is glorified racketeering. You have to have insurance, but then if you actually *use* it, they bump your rates up or drop you, despite the fact you've paid premiums for ten years."

Agent Petrocelli audibly sighed.

"What?"

"I can see it's going to be an uphill battle to win you over."

"Win me over? What do you care what I think of you?"

"I care. I don't know, I just do."

"If it makes you feel any better, I don't hate the police

and the FBI. Well, not totally. I hate that there's a lot of hy-pocrisy surrounding some of what you do. A 'win at any cost' mentality."

"Why don't you pretend I sell shoes?"

"Shoes?"

"Yeah. Shoes. And I've just called you up, and we're just having a conversation."

"About what?"

"I don't know. How was your day?"

"Long and tiring. Quinn wants me to write a cookbook."

"Sounds like a good idea."

"Yes. But the whole concept is that it will be Marcello family recipes. I've never capitalized on the Marcello name before."

"I bet they're good recipes, though. With a last name like mine…I know good Italian food. My grandmother makes a veal meatball that is not to be believed. Maybe I should do a cookbook. *A Shoe Salesman's Collection of Recipes.*"

"Instant bestseller. Actually, my recipes are really good. Delicious, wonderful recipes full of my aunts' teasing and my uncles' posturing—full of memories, I guess. Full of love. Any Italian will tell you that's the best ingredient."

"So maybe you should do it."

"Maybe. I'm thinking about it. And how was your day?"

"Well, if I was a foot fetishist, it would have been a great day, but I'm not, so you know, it was tiring. Women come in all day long, ask to see fifteen different pairs of shoes in their size. They ask me if their ankles look fat. I tell them no, but still at the end of the day, they don't buy anything, and I just have to restock five hundred pairs of shoes."

"Doesn't sound like a very good job. Unless you're a foot fetishist." I couldn't help smiling.

"Exactly."

"Do you have any other fetishes?" As soon as I said it, I blushed. What was I doing engaging in late-night small talk murmurings with an enemy of the house of Marcello? Quinn was the risk-taker, not me.

"Afraid not. Unless you count having a thing for seeing a woman laugh."

"What kind of a fetish is that? Is it naked laughing?"

"No. Not naked. Just laughing. Not polite sort of laughing. I'm talking gales of laughter, 'tears streaming down a woman's face' laughter."

"And that would be sexy how?" Whenever I laughed like that, I got a runny nose.

"I don't know. It's just so real. I guess that's what it's all about. Like going on a date with a woman who orders the most expensive thing on the menu but then won't eat. What is that? It's fucking lobster! Excuse my language."

"Please. I think we're all baptized with the word fuck as our middle name in the Marcello and Gallo clans…. And I know about those women you're talking about. I know the type. Happens all the time at Teddi's. Then we give them doggie bags, but I know all my hard work is going to end up in someone's trash can. We have a veal dish—very pricey. Why order it if you're only going to have two bites?"

"Yeah. It's the battle of the real women versus the fake women. I like down-to-earth. Real…and no one laughed at the shoe store today."

"Sorry to hear that. Must have been a very lonely day."

"It was. So I called you. What are you watching?"

"Law & Order."

"Hmm. I hate cops. I don't know why, being as I'm an

honest shoe salesman. I shouldn't really hate them. And I have no reason to fear them. I suppose it's the hypocrisy I hate."

"Do you now?" I laughed. "Well, I don't mind television cops. I like Chris Noth. Reruns of him on *Law & Order*. He could arrest me."

"On what grounds?"

"Well, I have none. That's the thing. My parents are retired schoolteachers. My mom taught kindergarten, and my father taught high school biology. So…they're totally innocent of anything. Boring background, really. They couldn't get arrested for jaywalking in this town."

"I hear you. So Teddi…what are you wearing?"

"Why do men always ask you that when they call you late at night?"

"They like to picture you."

"I'm naked," I lied.

"You better watch that someone doesn't use a pair of binoculars to spy on you."

"A city of a million voyeurs. And I'm one of an anonymous zillion in this city. Who would be watching me?"

"You're right. Maybe some cop on a stakeout."

"I've never been on a stakeout. I hear the stakeouters drink a lot of coffee."

"I wouldn't know…. I should let you get some sleep."

"Okay. But make me laugh first."

"How?"

"I don't know. Amuse me."

So he told me a joke about a pair of Irish twins. I'd heard it before. Quinn knew every Irish joke in the universe—and every Italian and Polish joke, too—but hearing Mark tell it made me laugh. And then when I laughed, he did, too.

"You have a nice laugh, Teddi Gallo."

"So do you, Mark Petrocelli, shoe salesman."

"See?" he whispered.

"See what?"

"How simple life would be?"

"Yeah," I whispered. "Good night."

"Sleep tight. Keep your windows locked."

"I will."

" 'Night Teddi."

" 'Night."

"Teddi?"

"Yeah?"

"You're Italian, right? I mean kindergarten and biology teacher parents, but Italian, right?"

"And half Sicilian. And you?"

"Italian. I gotta ask you, Teddi…do you believe in the thunderbolt?"

I didn't say anything. I looked over at all the silver frames on my table. Mariella and Uncle Mario were there, from back when Mariella was the most beautiful woman in all of Brooklyn.

"Teddi? You there?"

I didn't trust my voice, so I cleared my throat and finally said, "Yeah…I'm here."

"So do you?"

"I don't know."

"I do. Good night."

"Good night."

I hung up the phone, my stomach spinning. I lifted my hand to my face to brush away my hair. My hand was trembling.

Maybe talking to the FBI *was* dangerous.

Or maybe Agent Mark Petrocelli made me long for something I didn't know I wanted.

The next morning, I heard Di get out of the shower and the sound of a blow-dryer humming. I pulled on my terry robe, opened my door and ran across the hall.

"Di…Di…" I tapped her on the shoulder and she screamed.

"What are you doing up? You scared me."

I stared incredulously at her. While blowing her hair dry, she was listening to a CD Walkman, hooked onto the elastic of her red satin underwear, headphones in her ears.

"Let me turn this off!" she said loudly. She turned off the blow-dryer, then removed her Walkman. I could hear the faint, tinny sound of George Michael.

"What are you doing? Turn it off completely."

"What does it look like I'm doing? I'm blow-drying my hair. It's supposed to dip below thirty today. I don't want to step out with damp hair."

"I mean the Walkman, Lady Di."

She looked at me as if I were the stupidest person on earth. "Listening to George Michael, of course. Stupid nitwit. I do this almost every morning. If you work a double, I don't want to wake you up with my stereo."

"And is it not, perhaps—and I'm just floating an idea here…like a trial balloon—is it *not* possible to get dressed for work *without* George Michael? Or, alternatively, with him on low volume?"

"You've got to be kidding me, Teddi. That would be like having sex without an orgasm. Like…eating bread without butter…like wearing a designer dress with Payless shoes… like—"

"I get it."

"You look a fright. A positive fright."

"Yeah, well, if I tell you something, you can't tell Tony."

"Oh, please, as if you have to ask me. I've taken the...you know...that vow of silence thingie."

"All right. Last night, at quarter to one, Special Agent Mark Petrocelli called me."

"James Bond called you? At home? At that hour?" Suddenly, without any warning, she began shrieking like a cheerleading wannabe who has suddenly learned she's made the team. She jumped up and down and hugged me. Then just as suddenly she seemed to think of something serious. "Oh, my word...he didn't call to arrest you, did he?"

"No. He called because...well, it was weird. It was about some Mafia stuff. He said he saw my light on." I decided Lady Di could not handle thinking Tony might be in danger. Better to let her get used to family business slowly.

"Well, that doesn't sound like a pleasant phone call."

"It was actually kind of sweet."

"Wonderful, darling! I am so happy for you. What else did you talk about?"

"Well, then he started saying wasn't it a shame we were from...you know...two different worlds. He said something like, 'Imagine if I sold women's shoes.' Some ordinary job like that."

"Hmm. Maybe he's a foot fetishist. I dated one of those."

"No, he's not. But we did just have this weird conversation where we sort of pretended to be people we're not. I mean, I was me, but I said my parents were teachers. And we just had this great late-night conversation."

"Teachers?"

"I knew this would be more trouble than it was worth. Di, forget all that. Focus on the important stuff. He called me. To talk sexy. Suffice it to say we spoke into the wee hours."

"Phone sex?"

"No. But sexy. Very sexy. When we said good night, we were positively whispering sweet nothings."

"How exciting!"

"But you forget that 1) I am already dating Robert, and 2) Mark's an FBI agent, Di. If you thought Robert was the equivalent of me bringing Freddie Krueger home to meet the parents, imagine me bringing home a man with a badge."

"First of all, you're not dating Robert exclusively. Neither one of you has said anything about that. You can have both. You're a chef. Life is a smorgasbord. Why make do with a red plate special?"

"Blue plate."

"Fine. Blue. Red. Have it your way."

"Because it's not my style."

"Well…there is a chemistry between you and James Bond."

"I don't want to admit you're right. But you are, and I can't figure out why. Is it forbidden fruit?"

"What? Like he's a giant kiwi or something?"

"You know. That Romeo and Juliet thing?"

"No, Teddi. I have known you eight years now, and you are never like this. Plus, you've met cops before. Remember that blind date?"

"A disaster. But the whole thing is it can never, never work. So I just have to hope he never calls me again. There're just too many obstacles. Besides, from his side of things, what he's doing is probably illegal."

"Perfect!"

"Perfect?"

"Don't you get it? It means he bends the rules. Your family bends the rules. You're not so terribly different, after all."

"Di, I think Wham! has massaged your brain for the last time. When my family bends the rules, it means twenty phones in the basement."

"Well, why should anyone care how many telephone lines a person has? This is a free country. Or at least it's supposed to be. In England they don't care how many telephones you have. I bet Queen Elizabeth has a hundred phone lines in Buckingham Palace. Maybe two hundred."

"Diana, the queen isn't taking *book!* Telephone lines— that many—are a sure sign of being a bookie. So, Exhibit A: the Marcellos. Bookies. Loansharks. Break a few legs. Bury a few bodies. Have intimate knowledge of Jimmy Hoffa's demise. Exhibit B: Special Agent Mark Petrocelli. Fed haircut. Goes on surveillance. Gets his jones on for a girl and calls her late at night. These are not equal rule-breakings. One side is very, very extreme. And one is very, very mild."

"Exactly what I said. Perfect match."

"I give up. You don't listen to a thing anyone says, do you."

"No. Of course not. I am very happy for you, darling."

I shook my head and went back to my room to crash. If my father thought Robert Wharton was "wormy," I could just imagine what sort of twelve-word expletive-filled diatribe would fly from his mouth if he ever heard his daughter had become infatuated with an FBI agent.

chapter 15

"Boss, you look like somethin' my brother once saw hiding in the subway."

"Thanks so much, Leon."

"I mean it. Somebody saw you in my neighborhood they'd take you back out in the alley and shoot you."

"Again, thank you. You know how to make a girl feel special. And I must say, your own bald head is needing a bit of a shave tonight."

He ran his hand over his head. He was done cooking for the day. "Nah, boss lady, I'm growin' out my hair."

"Growing it out, are we?"

"Yup. Me and Chef Jeff. We decided to grow dreads together."

"Together? Leon...Jeff has stringy blond hair."

"You wash it with salt water. It'll get good and dread."

"Wonderful. What a pair you two will be. And you think *I* look like something hiding in the subway?"

"Yeah. And you look sad, too. What's wrong?"

"Nothing, Leon."

"Hey, Luis. Don't she look b-a-a-a-d today?" He said *bad* in the way my mother does, with multiple syllables.

Luis looked at me with his remaining good eye and nodded. "Very bad. Very, very bad, man."

I lifted a small cleaver I used to cut pieces of meat. "Leon, get out of my kitchen or I'll shave your head with this."

He held up his hands. "All right, boss lady. All right. And by the way…Cammie quit today."

"What?"

"Quinn's called in Angela, some girl he knows, to cover. But I better tell you—not like you won't figure it out when you lay eyes on this bitch. Angela works at a titty bar."

"A what?"

"A titty bar. You know, naked ladies."

"I know what a titty bar is. I'm just in shock! This is great. Fucking great."

Leon left the kitchen, and I put down my meat cleaver. If I had it in my hand, I was sure to hurl it at Quinn. I inhaled deeply and went to the front of the restaurant.

Quinn was behind the bar and already had his hands up as I came storming at him. "I know what you're going to say already, Teddi, but save it. We have a lot to do to get ready for tonight. I'm not going to fight with you now."

"Quinn…I mean it. You do this again and I'm through. I can't keep watching you do this."

Out of the corner of my eye, I noticed a woman putting down silverware.

"Tell me…" I seethed. "Tell me that is not Angela. Tell me. Fucking tell me to my face that is not our waitress."

"Yes, yes. Now shut up and stay in the kitchen."

"Give me a shot of whiskey. I'm going to need it tonight."

He poured me the shot, I downed it in a flash and stormed back to the kitchen, passing Angela with her size 48DD breasts prancing from table to table.

There is a saying in the restaurant business. When you're busy, you're "in the weeds." Well, we were weeded. Beyond weeded. Ju–Ju-B and I put out dinner after dinner, never so much as stopping to wipe the sweat off our brows or take a glass of water or soda. I couldn't see past the weeds. I was like Jimmy Hoffa in the Meadowlands. Overgrown.

Ju–Ju-B didn't like the hip-hop station that Leon liked. Chef Jeff was partial to heavy metal, but Ju–Ju-B liked reggae. And so, we cooked Italian to Bob Marley and tried to get out of the weeds.

Occasionally Quinn came back to see how stacked up we were, but he never said anything to me. He just looked repentant. Kept giving me these sad eyes I knew would be dancing the minute he was off work and in the sack with Angela or whoever.

Finally, around ten o'clock, I got my first chance to catch my breath. And that's when Quinn came in and said, "There's some guy here to see you."

I went over to one of the pots and looked at my distorted reflection in a lid. Poor Robert was going to be in for a shock. My face was flushed from the heat of the stove, my hair had curled to epic proportions and strained at its bobby pins. And I had circles under my eyes from my late-night discussion with Mark Petrocelli, after which I could not fall asleep.

"Here goes nothing," I said to Ju–Ju-B. "If he likes me after tonight, he's definitely a keeper."

I stepped out into the restaurant, tables down to three four-tops and two two-tops finishing up over coffee. And there at the bar sat Mark Petrocelli. I thought I would throw up from nerves at the sight of him.

I walked across the floor, feeling self-conscious in my stained chef coat, and smiled. "Hi," I said, and extended my hand.

"Hi."

I noticed he was nursing a club soda.

"Can I get you a real drink or are you on duty? Here to harass me or just for a visit?"

"No. Came off my shift selling shoes. I'll take a Glenfiddich if you have it. On the rocks."

Tatiana must have gone to the ladies' room, so I went behind the bar and poured him his Scotch.

"Here you go. Why are you here?"

"I wanted to try the food. A little bird told me this place has great food. What do you recommend?"

"We have a nice Florentine chicken."

"Sounds good. You look great, by the way."

I stared at him. Was he on drugs? No, they screened FBI agents for that. He wore a dark blue suit. "So do you." Only he really did.

I went back to the kitchen, praying my knees wouldn't fail me. "Ju-Ju-B, clean your station and then you can go home. This is probably the last dinner of the night."

"Okay, Teddi. Hey…you think that Angela would go out with me?"

"Anything's possible, Ju-Ju. Anything's possible. But I gotta tell ya, if you fuck her, please don't let me know about it."

"Deal."

Ju-Ju-B cleaned his work area and went to the front of the house. I peeked out the kitchen door and sure enough, Angela seemed to be leaving with him, God help us all.

I cooked Mark's chicken, feeling shaky and unsure of myself. Quinn came back into the kitchen.

"Who is this guy now?"

"Don't ask."

"I'm asking."

"Why?"

"First of all, I like him better than the TV repairman. At least he has good taste in alcohol. And second, I don't think I have ever seen you so unnerved by anyone in your life, and I think that's good for a person once in a while. I sent Tatiana home and the busboys are breaking down the tables. Why don't you eat dinner with your friend? He looks like a cop…but I don't even care. You like him. I can tell."

"In case you haven't noticed, it is the end of a totally weeded shift, and I *arrived* looking like hell and can assure you I know my appearance didn't *improve* over the course of the night. And as it is, I'm not talking to you."

Quinn moved closer to me. "You just did. We're made up. I'm sorry. I fucked up. But you're my best friend and my best cousin. Don't stay mad. Eat with your friend."

"And let you tease me? I don't think so."

"I promise I won't."

"Why? So I'll let you off the hook?"

"No. Because even if I do all my thinking with my dick, I can spot the real deal between two people when it comes along. Go. I mean it. And you don't look that bad. Though I'd lose the smear of tomato sauce on your chin."

"Great." I rubbed at my chin.

"And the piece of garlic in your hair."

Quinn reached out and pulled out the garlic. Then he tilted my chin until I looked at him.

"Gimme another chance, Teddi." He kissed the end of my nose.

I sighed in answer.

"Love you." He leaned in and kissed me on the cheek.

I ended up cooking two portions of dinner and brought them out after unloosing my hair from its losing battle with a bobby-pinned bun.

"Dinner is served, sir." I set the plates down on a two-top in the corner by the bar.

"I don't know when I have seen a woman in a more stylish outfit. The women who came into the shoe store today should take a cue from you."

I laughed. I was wearing steel-toed black boots in case I ever dropped a heavy can on my foot. I once broke two toes when I wore sneakers, and learned my lesson and copied Leon and Ju-Ju-B. In shoes, at least, we looked like refugees from a neo-Nazi gang. My coat was a mess. A testament to "the weeds." I went behind the bar and poured myself a glass of white wine and then joined Mark.

"And I smell like garlic, not some expensive perfume. Maybe they'll take a cue from that, too."

"I like a woman who smells like garlic. My last name is Petrocelli, after all."

"That's right. I'd almost forgotten."

"How could you forget me? I sure as hell can't forget you. In fact, the most annoying thing is all day long down at that shoe store, every time my mind wanders, it's wandering to you."

"Sure. I bet. I hear shoe salesmen are dedicated to their jobs 24/7."

"Well, you can pledge your mind to the shoe business, but not your heart." He plucked the purple flower in the bud vase on the table and said, "Allow me?"

I nodded, and he leaned over and tucked the flower into my hair.

"Perfect."

"Goes with the sauce on my coat, don't you think?"

"No. It goes with your hair. You have the kind of hair a man could get lost in."

"Yeah, but it's exceedingly difficult to get a comb through it."

"I like it just the way it is."

"Mark. You realize this is truly insane, don't you? Couldn't you be fired for consorting with the enemy or something?"

He nodded. "The home office of the shoe store—they're based in Peoria—they frown on this sort of thing."

"So why risk it?"

"I have a story to tell you."

"I'm listening." I sipped my wine, allowing myself to relax a little bit. It was only a meal, I told myself.

"My grandfather was once walking down the street...now, my Pops—that's what I call him—he is a guy who tells tall tales. You never know whether to believe him or not. You know, so much braggadocio."

"I think I know the type."

"He was dressed for mass on a Sunday when he was fifteen, and as he was walking to church, he sees this girl walking with *her* family to church. She's got like ten brothers, she's the only girl. Just her. No mother—he found out later her mother died. And her father, a nice man. Ran the local candy store. And Pops looks across the street and at that pre-

cise moment, she looked across the street and their eyes met.
And he was a goner. Struck by the thunderbolt."

"Aah...so that's why you asked. You know, the thunderbolt isn't always a good thing."

"Not so. Not so. Pops worked hard for two years—three
jobs—saved every penny he had, and he and his older
brother bought an appliance store. He also went to the track,
won a few races and soon he had a respectable bit of money
to ask the girl's father if he could have her hand in marriage."

"And?"

"She was sworn to another. But the girl was miserable.
She stopped eating. She locked herself in her room. Unbe-
knownst to the family, Pops had figured out a way to write
to his beloved by leaving her notes in the schoolyard under
a rock by a tree, and she left him notes in return.... She was
the apple of her father's eye, and in the end, her father
worked it out, and my grandmother and grandfather married—and are still together to this day. They live with my
aunt, and have a room...and two rockers side by side on the
front porch. And he's still a character...puts a flower in her
hair every morning."

"Has anyone ever told you that for a shoe salesman you're
a hopeless romantic?"

"No. Because I don't tell my thunderbolt story to just
anyone."

I touched the flower in my hair and took another sip
of wine.

"Is this the same grandfather who gambled away the family fortunes and caused your father to become a cop?"

Mark nodded. "But I was always torn between the ro-
mance of the gambler and the guy who bent the rules, and
the father who walked the straight and narrow."

"I suppose I've always been torn between loving my family and being loyal to them, and moving to New Zealand, because I would have to live on the other side of the earth to get away from them."

"What's your favorite ice cream?"

"What?"

"Just trying to get to know everything about you. As a shoe salesman, I don't get to practice my interviewing skills much, but I can try."

"Peppermint stick."

"Mine's chocolate. Okay, favorite football team?"

"Are you a native New Yorker?"

He nodded.

"Then it seems to me, Mark, you don't have to ask."

"Giants."

"Of course."

"Care to make a wager on Sunday's game?"

"I thought shoe salesmen didn't gamble?"

"I consider this a friendly bet. If the Giants cover the point spread, you have to cook dinner for me. If they don't, I have to cook dinner for you."

"I—I don't know."

"Come on. You can't really lose either way because I make a mean shrimp scampi—and if you have to cook, I promise to do the dishes."

"All right, then."

He smiled and then said, "We better eat or this meal's going to get cold."

Somehow, we made it through the entire rest of the meal without ever mentioning the Marcellos, the Gallos, the FBI, illegal bookmaking, or even good and evil. We simply ate, and laughed. A lot.

By the time we were through with our meal, the place was empty. Quinn came over to the table with two sambucas.

"Compliments of the house." He set them on the table. He stuck his hand out. "Quinn Gallo."

"Mark Petrocelli…nice to meet you."

"Teddi…back door's locked. Alarm on. Lock up front when you leave. I'm off to meet Tatiana."

I looked up at him.

"No, no. Don't act all pissy. What you said the other day made sense. I just hadn't seen it."

"Quinn, not Tatiana—"

He put his hands up. "Enjoy your sambuca."

He left and turned the volume up slightly on the Andrea Bocelli CD playing in the background.

"You ever think about leaving New York?" Mark asked me. "Opening a place somewhere else?"

I shook my head. "New York's in my blood. Kind of like cooking. Kind of like Quinn. He's hopeless, but I think I'm stuck with him. What about you?"

"Nah. I'm a New Yorker, too. Hooked on my bagel and schmear."

"You may be a New Yorker, but you have this Gary Cooper sensibility. This Midwestern white-hat cowboy thing going on."

He shrugged. "I like to help people."

"Buy shoes."

"Exactly," he nodded. "I feel like if I leave the world a bit better…by all those women finding the shoes of their dreams, making sure any bad shoes are shipped back to the factory…well, then I've had a good day."

"And a bad day is what?"

"When someone comes in with pinched toes and blisters and says I sold her the wrong pair."

We finished our drinks, the coffee beans now stuck to the bottom of our snifters.

"Mark…you know—" I stood up "—I have to lock this place up and head home."

"I understand." He suddenly looked uncomfortable. "Best food I ever tasted. You should do that cookbook."

"I just might."

"How are you getting home?"

"Tony will be here in about twenty minutes to take me home. He won't say what's up, but I know something is. I don't think you should be here when he gets here."

"Lock the door behind me."

"I will."

"Thanks for a fantastic meal."

"You're welcome."

He fumbled for his wallet.

"No, no, no. On the house."

"Thanks." He looked up at me and deposited his wallet in his back pocket again.

"Mark?"

"Yeah?"

"I really liked our phone call last night. And our dinner tonight. But you and I both know you don't sell shoes. Never did, never will—I bet you didn't even put yourself through college as a shoe salesman. And we both know that my grandfather has a long and colorful history…almost as long and colorful as the history of this city."

"I know. I accept that."

"You do, but you have to see this through to its logical conclusion. So I think maybe this should be the last time you come in here to eat. If you put me under surveillance, I can't help that. But this—whatever this is—just can't be. And we'd be really stupid to pretend otherwise. No matter what it is that seems to pass between us when we see each other."

"But you made a bet with me."

"And it was crazy of me to do that. Not just for my sake, but for your sake. You have your entire career to think of."

He nodded and came over close to me. Then, without any warning, he grabbed me fiercely and kissed me. He pulled on my hair; it was a hungry, strong, aching kiss. And then he pulled away.

"Goodbye, Teddi." He turned and left.

With tears in my eyes, I locked the door of the restaurant behind him. I took our two plates back to the kitchen to the sink. Almost as without warning as his kiss had been, tears started streaming down my face. I brushed them away and willed myself to be strong. To be a Gallo. A Marcello. Hell, I felt so bad, I didn't care which side had the tougher genes at that point.

Later, Tony came to the door and knocked. I let him in.

"You ready?"

"Almost."

He went to the bar and poured himself a Ketel One and cranberry.

"What's with you?"

"Nothing."

"You look like shit, Teddi. Is it that guy? That Robert guy? 'Cause if he hurt you, Teddi, I swear I'll—"

"You know, Tony…sometimes life just happens. That's what you and the rest of the family don't understand. You

can't control the outcome of everything." My voice was
hoarse.

"Why not?"

"Because you can't. I finally have figured out that's what's
wrong with the lot of you."

"What?" He sipped his drink.

"Uncle Vito gets a line on a horse. Or a college-hoops
star who's maybe in a little too deep to his bookie. You all
bet the way you think the outcome's going to be. You win.
You, in effect, control the gamble. Poppy doesn't like the
way one of his neighbors keeps his house, you pay a visit
and persuade the gentleman in question to trim his hedges.
You control the neighborhood. And let's not even get into
controlling all the illegal stuff down the line. Control, control, control. But sometimes, people just have feelings and
you can't control them."

"Bullshit."

"What about you and Lady Di?"

"What about us?" He looked intensely at me.

"Have you thought about what would happen if she
went back to England? Or what would happen if her British earl of something-or-other father met you? What would
you tell him you do for a living? Huh, Tony?"

He stared down, grim-faced, into his drink, and swirled
the ice around.

"Exactly. What I had to say about my father my whole
life. A big 'I don't know.' So you can't control her and you,
and you can't control me."

"I love her, Teddi."

"I know." I pulled out my keys and walked over to the
door. He downed his drink. I set the alarm, and we went
outside.

"What am I going to do?" He looked at me.

"I don't know. Because we can't control the outcome. We have to learn to play the game the way everyone else does. Like riding your bike downhill with your hands off the handlebars."

I climbed into the Town Car and Tony drove me home. Michel the doorman escorted me to the lobby. I turned to wave to Tony. He waved back, his face lonely-looking.

We were all riding downhill, and no one was steering.

chapter 16

On Thursday, Robert phoned me at work. He wanted me to meet Jerry Turner.

"Informal," Robert said. "You know. Just drinks. I want him to meet you.... Jerry and I are good friends, as well as colleagues. I think you'd like him. He's really a decent guy."

"That's what my father says about Louie 'Knuckles' Bastone."

"Isn't he serving life in Sing Sing?"

"My point exactly."

"You want to compare a cold-blooded killer, who allegedly kept a collection of eyeballs next to his finger collection in jars on his mantel—"

"Nothing alleged about it. I saw the fingers once."

"You want to compare this man with Jerry Turner, the television journalist?"

"Yes. I do."

"Teddi…this isn't like you."

I felt tired of people telling me who I was. "Jerry Turner once said my uncle Teddy, my father's brother, was akin to the Son of Sam. *Son of Sam,* Robert. He isn't interested in truth. He's interested in ratings."

"Didn't your father's brother get convicted for murdering two men and chopping them into little pieces and burying them underneath the concrete patio of his restaurant?"

"He was framed. The concrete foreman did it."

Robert snorted into the phone.

"What was that?" I asked him.

"Teddi…look…please meet Jerry. He's a friend. You're both important to me."

"Fine. But discussion of my family is off-limits."

"Deal. Hey, why have you been hiding from me lately?"

"I'm not hiding."

"Well, you have been hard to track down."

"Just busy. Nature of the restaurant business." I softened. "I work a double shift some days. I work nights. Early mornings. It's a grueling business and not good for relationships. You're equally busy. That's all it is."

Jerry, Robert and I met at Whiskey Blue and were shown to a small table in the corner, away from the crowd at the bar. The waitress, who weighed about eighty pounds, tops, and who wore a black leotard and miniskirt with thigh-high boots, fawned over Jerry Turner, leaning in extra close and squeezing what little breasts she had in her push-up bra together.

In person, Jerry Turner was less imposing than the man who bellowed live at the cameras five nights a week, with reruns on the weekends. He actually looked like a nice gentleman in a suit and tie, with a smile that made his eyes crinkle in the corners, and a big semipompadour of silvery-blond hair swept back from his forehead.

"I should thank you," he said to me after we ordered a round of drinks.

"Why?"

"Since he met you, Robert is a dream to work with. Always in a good mood."

I smiled at the compliment. "Well...I've been in a good mood since I met him, too."

"I trust Robert like the back of my hand. In my business, you can't say that about too many people."

"I hear you." Not too different from my family's business, where trust and loyalty were the most valued commodities of all.

The waitress, with a mop of curly blond hair on her head, which resembled a Q-Tip atop her thin frame, brought us our drinks, and I sipped my martini.

"Do you watch the show?" Jerry asked me, raising his voice slightly over the music.

Robert looked nervously at me.

"Not really. I actually don't watch a lot of television."

"Everyone says that. Come on. I'm a big boy. I can take it. You don't like me, do you. I don't mean personally. I mean...the whole show. The TV me." The TV him had just gotten off the air a half hour before. He still had makeup on.

"Well..." I took a sip. "You're a little confrontational. But Robert says you're very dedicated to finding out the truth."

"Absolutely." He slapped my knee. "The truth and ratings. Hand in hand."

Robert laughed. "Jerry has the highest ratings of any cable show in the eight o'clock slot."

"Good for you." I smiled.

"I'll let you in on a little secret."

"What?"

"When Robert told me he was dating Don Angelo Marcello's granddaughter, well, you can imagine the thoughts that went through my head."

My smile tightened. Of course I could imagine. It was what everyone imagined my entire life.

"No, what?" I asked.

"Well…you know all the stereotypes."

Sure. They called me Teddi Tortellini when I was in grade school. The fact that my cousins could pulverize anyone who messed with me helped me more times than I cared to count. But after a while, I was avoided as if I had "the cooties."

"Sure, Jerry. But I'm not my family."

"Something Robert here made very plain to me. Still, it had to have been interesting. Off the record. Come on…"

"'Interesting' would be a good way to describe it."

Interesting wasn't the half of it, of course. Other kids told stories of visits to grandma and grandpa's house, complete with cookie-baking and getting to stay up past bedtime. My fondest memories were of days at the track, learning to read racing forms. The fact that I could pick winners better than any of my male cousins—except Quinn—was a badge of honor. I was Poppy's favorite—and everyone knew it.

"The RICO trial seven years ago must have been hard."

"The RICO Act is what the government gets you on when they've got nothing. They try to tie you to bullshit, Jerry. You know that as well as I do. They play connect the dots with nothing tangible. Notice they only got two convictions out of twenty-four indictments. And that was all for bullshit small-time stuff. My cousin did three months, my uncle Vito walked."

Jerry raised his Scotch and soda in a salute to me. "Your friend here is pretty tough, Robert. She's no pushover. Not that I'd guess Angelo Marcello's granddaughter would be."

Robert lifted his glass and winked at me. I downed the rest of my martini and bit an olive off the plastic toothpick.

Jerry was not one to give up. "Your grandfather still running things?"

"Running what things?" I asked.

"You know. The family."

"No. I don't know." For some reason, I liked making Jerry Turner have to say what was on his mind.

"Oh…I forgot. He's a restaurateur."

"Exactly."

Robert rubbed my forearm protectively. "Come on, let's talk about something else."

"All right. Are the Giants going to win on Sunday?" Jerry asked.

"Of course they are." I grinned but then immediately felt a rock in my stomach as I thought of sending away Mark. I had kept the flower from my hair. It dried out overnight, and I pressed it behind a picture frame.

"I think they might go all the way this year," Jerry mused.

"Please," I said. "The Giants toy with their fans every year. They make us think they're going all the way and then they blow it. I miss Bill Parcells. He took us to the Super Bowl in 1981 and 1987. But I root for the stupid Giants, anyway."

"A woman after my own heart," Jerry said. "You care to place a wager on Sunday?"

"Depends."

"I say they don't cover the spread."

"I say they do."

"Fifty bucks."

"You're on." We shook on it.

The three of us then moved on to a discussion of restaurants and hot spots and life in Manhattan. I started to relax. I felt like we'd moved past the novelty of my family. That's all I asked for—a chance to be seen as Teddi, as myself. Robert saw me that way. Lady Di did, too. Mark Petrocelli did—and he didn't. At the same time, I liked to bait people like Jerry who met me with their own preconceived notions.

Somewhere around twelve-thirty, we called it a night and waited as the doorman in front of the W Hotel called us two cabs. Robert and Jerry took one, and I took the other.

"I'll call you tomorrow," Robert whispered as he kissed me. I had been replaying the kiss with Mark in my mind, but Robert was sensual. Nothing wrong with his kisses, either.

"Talk to you then." I smiled as I slipped into the cab.

On the ride home, I settled against the seat and looked at New York, alive at night, as the cabbie whizzed me past restaurants and all-night delis and coffee shops. I gazed up at the apartment buildings, glimpsing people as they moved about their apartments. New York City is a voyeur's paradise. It reminded me of the old dioramas we had to make in grade school, little frozen scenes, a flash of a person at a window, doing dishes at the kitchen sink. Another apartment might have the bluish tint of the television reflecting off the windows. People stood hailing cabs. Little poodles and shih tzus and Pekingese with their pushed-in faces were walked by their owners. Occasionally, you saw a dog walker handling five or more dogs at once. I loved the anonymity. I loved Manhattan.

The cabbie pulled in front of my apartment building, and I paid the fare and tipped the driver.

"Good night," I said, then slid out and held open the door for a couple who hurried over to seize the cab.

The night doorman, Michel, waved to me and held open the door to the building.

"*Bonjour,* Teddi."

"*Bonjour,* Michel. How's Gabriella?" I inquired after his wife. "She have that baby yet?"

"No. Not yet. Mrs. Weiss in 9C told me I should take her out for Mexican food. The spicy food will start contractions, she says. You think that'll work?"

"I think that baby, Michel, will come when he's good and ready. But you never know. It's worth a try. You know, there's a place over on Eighty-eighth called the Orange Blossom. It has some kind of salad with a patented balsamic dressing. Was a cute article in one of the papers how it started labor for three mothers in one week."

"We'll try anything." Michel smiled at me, and walked to the elevator.

"Good luck," I said. I got on the elevator and made a mental note to ask Di to go shopping with me on Saturday to buy some baby outfits for Michel and his wife.

I unlocked my apartment and stepped inside. Di wasn't home, and I walked back to my bedroom and slipped out of my shoes and clothes and put on pajamas.

I felt tired. Maybe what I wanted was instant understanding. I wanted to skip the getting-to-know-you phase and move right into acceptance. I didn't want to recount every detail of my life from puberty to the RICO trials and beyond. I didn't want people to judge me. And suddenly, I wished more than anything that Special Agent Mark Petrocelli really did sell shoes.

chapter 17

Pip left a message on my machine in his super-squeaky, always an octave higher than you thought a man could speak in, voice. The news was not good: "Theresa, you will not make payroll this month. I told Quinn this, but he seems to think he can...charm the numbers. He can't. Numbers are numbers, Theresa. I need to talk to you. You're the only sane one there."

My head pounded. The cash wasn't really an issue. Quinn and I both had savings, and we knew surviving in a city with a restaurant on every corner was not going to be easy. We planned for months like this. Well, I planned for them, and I *forced* Quinn to plan for them. But I also knew an infusion of cash was only a quick fix. Once you started infusing your business with cash for the payroll, you'd be infusing it month after month after month. And before too long, you were another bankrupt restaurant.

Much as I hated to say it, maybe it was time I met with

Lady Di and her literary agent friend. One Sunday, Lady Di
had even mentioned it to the aunts, who all thought it was
a great idea. They envisioned their names above recipes.
"Aunt Gina's Pasta Primavera." But associating Teddi's with
the mob was never what I had in mind. I wanted Quinn and
I to make it on our own. But in reality, we had borrowed
the money from family to start with, anyway, so "on our
own" was just a matter of definition. I was trying to reason
with myself, to tell myself it was okay to "cheat" a little bit
and to put the family name to real use. In truth, my entire
life it had been a hardship, and if now it turned out to be
an advantage, maybe that was all right.

I mentioned the idea to Lady Di when she came into my
room in the morning to borrow a clean towel. Neatness and
laundry—neither was her strong suit. At the mention of the
cookbook, she was characteristically ecstatic.

"You'll love this woman. She's a genius! And think of it.
You could end up a famous author. You know that 'Nigella
Bites' lady—Nigella Lawson?"

"She's British. And a chef. And beautiful."

"Yes. But Nigella bites what? A penis? I think you can
come up with a great cookbook title. And a great cookbook."

That morning, when Quinn came in, I told him that
Anna Friedman and Lady Di were coming to lunch and I
was seriously considering doing a cookbook after all.

"You won't regret it, little cuz. When we're on a three-
hour wait every night, it'll be so worth it."

Did I really want to be weeded every night? If Lady Di's
scheme worked, we'd have to hire more help in the kitchen.
Let alone the front of the house. And Lord only knew if
there was a waitress left in Manhattan who would consider

working for Quinn. I knew he saw dollar signs, women and fame. I saw more work in the kitchen…and, all right, four stars next to a review of the restaurant.

Nervously, I cooked lunch for Lady Diana and Anna Friedman. Then I left Chef Jeff in charge of the kitchen while I went out front to talk with them. Chef Jeff's budding, so-called dreads looked seriously disgusting. He hid them under a red bandanna.

Up front, I sat down with Lady Di and Anna. Both women were in power suits, but Diana looked feminine. The cut of her suit was softer, and a colorful Hermès scarf framed her face. Her shoes were sexy and five inches tall. Anna, on the other hand, looked like a Russian Afghan hound in heels. Her face was pinched, and framed by long hair, and though Di told me she was thirty-four, she looked about forty-four, the way she carried herself and with her severe makeup (bright red lipstick you could spot from the other side of the room, and pale, pale skin).

I sat down, a bit uneasy. Anna started talking in a rapid machine-gun-fire staccato. Question after question:

How old was my grandfather?
How long had my family been on American shores from Italy?
Did I go to culinary school or was I self-taught?
Were these authentic Marcello and Gallo family recipes?
Could we do photo shoots in the restaurant?
How quickly could I pull together my recipes?
How many recipes did I have?
Would any real "Mafia people" agree to be in photographs?

The woman barely took a breath in between each question. No sooner had I spat out an answer that she was on to the next one, but you could see her mentally calculating the very next question, not really listening to what I was saying. She unnerved me. Finally, head swimming, I told Lady Di I needed to use the ladies' room.

"I'll come, too," Di said.

Once we were alone in the stairway leading down to the bathrooms, Di cornered me. "Well?"

"She's a horror show. My God, but she's evil! Evil!"

"That's what you want. You want a six-figure deal, don't you? You want someone who is tough as nails at the negotiating table. That is what you want."

"Maybe…" I said hesitantly. "But…"

"You don't look yourself, Teddi. You seem off your game."

"James Bond kissed me the other night."

"What? How could you withhold such vital information from me?

"Because I told him I could never see him again."

"Fool! He's the one for you."

"Robert is."

"Poppycock!"

"Can we please stay focused on the book here?"

"I think you should do it."

"I don't know." We went into the ladies' room and washed our hands and conferred some more.

"Maybe I would be better off with a literary agent who isn't like Eva Braun up there."

"You want Eva. You want a deal. Come on. Let's go back up."

When we ascended the staircase and came out into the

restaurant, there was Quinn, sitting down with Anna, and she was laughing like a giddy schoolgirl. I should have seen it coming.

"Oh, Teddi, you didn't tell me your partner was so charming. And so photogenic, I bet. Well…I've certainly seen that this cookbook idea is a winner. Let's shake on it, shall we?"

I looked at Quinn, who batted his eyes at me and grinned. "Like the beautiful lady says, it's a winner, Teddi."

I looked at Lady Di. Her eyes were imploring. She considered the task of doing PR for Teddi's to be her pet project. She was itching to do it.

The thought of Pip's voice hounding me for payroll echoed in my mind. That whiny voice.

I found myself sticking out my hand.

And then I heard my voice: "It's a deal."

At Sunday dinner, I mentioned that I was going to do a cookbook of Marcello family recipes. My aunts were elated. They spent much of the day scribbling on a pad of yellow paper all the various bits of Marcello cooking advice they could think of, including some recipes. We all agreed we'd never reveal the secret to my grandmother's wonderful pasta fajoli, as that recipe was sacred to us all, and we didn't feel right sharing it with the public.

Poppy Marcello even seemed pleased that a book would leave a "legacy." He took me aside.

"This is a good thing, Teddi Bear. Your grandmother— she woulda been proud. You make the family proud. *Capisce?*"

The more I thought about it, the more comfortable I got with the idea. When Quinn and I had opened Teddi's, I envisioned a place that would make the critic from the *New*

York Times give us four stars. In the end, we were too much a small neighborhood place to attract the *Times* critic, so my goal became to make us famous in the neighborhood. To cultivate regulars who loved our food. And we had done that. In our own little sphere, our own little neighborhood world, which was the way New York City life was, we were a four-star restaurant. We had Mr. and Mrs. Goldfarb, who came in every Tuesday night for dinner; the Mangione sisters, two spinsters who ate there on Thursday lunch and always gave the busboy, Javier, a dollar because he reminded them of their little brother when they had all been children. There was Tommy Korn, aka, Tommy Special-K, a professional wrestler who swore my pasta gave him just the carb loading he needed. And every time one of the regulars walked through the door, Quinn smiled and treated them like kings and queens of a small nation. I loved what we had become, and if a cookbook let us stay open, let us grow, then I would do it.

"Hey Teddi!" My uncle Vito shouted down the table.

"Yes, Uncle V.?"

"Next week, your boyfriend still taking us to the Giants game?"

"Yes, Uncle V." I noticed no one, including myself, ever answered questions in a normal tone of voice. It was always "yes" or "no" with a New York weariness. It was how we spoke to one another.

"We'll have a good time. Good time. The Giants could go to the Bowl, you know. To the Big One."

"Yes, I know."

Simultaneously three of my aunts and assorted cousins and uncles made the sign of the cross. The Giants being in the Super Bowl not only meant the bookie business would be very good, but it was something akin to a trifecta at the Kentucky Derby—actually, to a miracle at Lourdes. In short, we lived and breathed the Giants, and more than a few rosaries were said on their behalf…though I can tell you a few of their seasons had clearly shown all the rosaries in the world weren't helping them any.

"Now, listen, you all." I banged on my water glass with my spoon to get their attention. "Be easy on the poor guy, okay?"

"No problem." Uncle Vito smiled. "We'll treat him real good."

"That's what I'm afraid of."

"No need to be afraid, Theresa," my uncle Lou said. "If he has treated you like the princess you are, then he has nothing to fear from us."

I felt relieved. "He has been nothing but a gentleman, and he has treated me very, very well."

"See then?" my father said, using up two words and then a whole stream of them. "Your boyfriend has nothing to worry about."

"Why—" I rolled my eyes heavenward "—do I find myself worrying, anyway?"

That night, my phone rang around ten-thirty.

"You owe me dinner," Mark's voice teased over the telephone.

"The Giants game today."

"A bet's a bet. You wouldn't want word getting out to the bookies that you're not good for your bets, would you?"

"I think that's the least of my worries about now."

"I'm putting in for a transfer, Teddi."

"To where?" I felt a panic rising up in my throat.

"Another division. I think you wise guys are just a little too much for me."

"What kind of division?"

"White-collar crime. I get to go after inside traders and corrupt CEOs. I kind of like the idea of putting away the millionaires who fuck over the little guy."

"Will you leave New York?"

"Nah. Not me. If I moved away I wouldn't get to go to my new favorite restaurant. Ever hear of it? A little place called Teddi's. You know what I love about it most?"

I guessed he was going to say something adorable like "the chef," but I was wrong.

"The pictures."

"What pictures?"

"In the bar. You have to see them all. Pictures of Ellis Island and the Statue of Liberty. Pictures of family. Pictures of lovers and husbands and wives with a half-dozen kids around them. Pictures. That's what I like."

"I didn't think anyone noticed."

"I noticed."

"You're really complicating my life, Mark."

"Yeah, princess, you ain't exactly making mine easier, either."

"I should go."

"Dinner? When?"

"Let me straighten out a few things, Mark. I have your card."

"Use it."

"You'll be the first to know when I'm ready for a new pair of shoes."

chapter 18

I needed to make a decision. Thunderbolt FBI agent or reliable but extremely handsome, sincere and attentive TV journalist. On Tuesday, hoping to figure out this mess once and for all, I decided to invite Robert over for dinner and to cook him an old-fashioned Italian meal. I didn't work from a cookbook, but from an old, dog-eared index card with the Marcello family gravy recipe written on it in my grandmother's shaky handwriting. Even at that, it wasn't like any recipe most people have ever followed. For instance:

Pour some olive oil in a big pot. The biggest you can find. Cook some garlic in it. A lot of garlic. But not the jar stuff—the real stuff.
Add four big cans of tomatoes. Season with oregano. Not too much, not too little.
Taste. Add more.

Add pepper and salt. Taste.
Add a little red wine. Doesn't have to be good stuff.
Taste.

And the recipe went on and on. Lots of tasting involved.
No measurements. No indication of when it was done.
Making gravy was an all-day affair. Not surprising, with all
that tasting, by the time dinner actually arrived, I never felt
much like eating. It was almost like a built-in diet. Little
tastes instead of a big calorie-laden meal. In fact, my hands
reeked of garlic, and if I never saw a tomato again it would
be too soon.

As I cooked, I took some notes. I would have to do some
serious calculations if I was ever to turn these dog-eared
index cards into real recipes that worked in a typical American kitchen.

Robert came over promptly at seven o'clock. Diana and
Tony were planning on going to a Broadway show since my
cousin Tony had never been to one. *Ever.* The closest my
cousin came to culture was watching A&E on occasion. Di
was wise to at least choose a musical. A serious play would
have put Tony over the edge.

Robert arrived while Di was in her room dressing. I
showed him to the living room, where the red roses he had
sent to work were displayed, just a touch wilted, and poured
him a glass of merlot.

"I'm putting the finishing touches on dinner."

"Smells out of this world."

"Thank you." I went back to the kitchen, which was
sickeningly hot. I opened the window and a rush of New
York City coldness whooshed through, raising goose bumps
on my arms.

I heard Diana emerge and greet Robert, and could hear their murmuring small talk. She came to the kitchen doorway, a vision of black velvet, and put on her coat to go downstairs to meet Tony.

"Don't wait up for me." She smiled, wrapping a cashmere scarf around her neck.

"I know better than to wait up for you. And when Tony sees you, he will definitely think that sitting through, in his words, 'a bunch of gay gays and some babes singing and dancing' will be worth it."

"Let's hope so. I'm slowly introducing him to a little culture. Though he's really very bright. Reads the *Wall Street Journal* every day. Did you know that?"

I shook my head.

"Is that garlic bread?"

I nodded.

"I'd have a piece, but I don't want garlic breath."

"I'm sure there'll be plenty left over."

Suddenly, her eyes watered.

"What?" I asked, closing the oven door.

"Be careful," she whispered.

"Of what?"

"Of him." She jerked her head in the direction of the living room.

"What do you mean?"

"I mean just be careful. You don't know much about him."

"Diana, this isn't like you."

She wiped at her eyes. "I know. I'm sorry." She rushed forward and kissed my cheek. "Maybe I was just hoping for the FBI agent. It's such a meet-cute story."

"Di-i-i…" I whined, sounding suspiciously like my mother and extending the single syllable into three.

"But think of the stories you could tell people of how you met."

"Diana, you've been a little odd before, but I always chalked it up to your British roots. Now I think you are just plain crazy. You don't date people so you can tell 'meet-cute' stories."

"I do…well, off I go."

"Enjoy the show."

"I will. And then the after-the-show." She winked at me.

Lady Di left the kitchen and then the apartment. I was completely bewildered by her rush of weird emotions. But then again, Diana had some sort of…*disorder* is the only word I can put to it. She could never focus.

I put the garlic bread into a basket and brought dinner out to the table. "Dinner is served," I said.

Robert got up from the couch. "Can I help you with anything?"

"No. I've pretty much got it under control."

"Wonderful." He sat down and put the napkin on his lap, and I sat opposite him.

Robert stared at me. "You look beautiful in candlelight, Teddi."

I blushed. "Garlic bread?" I passed the basket.

"So…did I pass your family's inspection?"

"Um, I think so. Of course, taking them to the Giants game will endear you more than anything else ever could."

"I thought so. Diehard New Yorkers. Next you'll have to meet my parents. They come to Manhattan several times a year. Stay at the Waldorf. Do the museum thing."

The museum thing. I would wager no one in my family had ever seen the inside of a museum.

"And what do you think your parents would say about me?"

"They'd think you were beautiful, smart. I think I'd wait

until they fell in love with you before telling them everything."

"Good thinking." I was used to waiting until just the right moment to discuss my family.

"Jerry Turner thinks you're amazing."

"Really?" Personally, I was underwhelmed by America's favorite muckraker.

"You know, he'd love to talk to you—off the record, of course—about this piece he's doing on the changing face of crime."

"Not a chance." I played with my spaghetti and nibbled on my garlic bread.

"What if I told you I was thinking of doing a piece on the unsolved Corelli murder?"

"I'd have no opinion."

My real opinion was a hybrid of panic and hysteria. Gino Cordelli had been gunned down outside his favorite restaurant in 1987. The person who stood to gain the most from his demise was Poppy Angelo. Since Corelli's murder was never solved, every amateur sleuth with a theory had expounded on how it happened and why. Other culprits were occasionally named. But, despite miles and miles of wiretap, I am sure, and more than a few people turned rat, no one had ever definitively pointed to my grandfather. I knew resentments between the Corellis and Marcellos ran deep.

"No opinion?" He lifted a big forkful of spaghetti to his mouth.

"None. So tell me, what's your favorite movie of all time?" I wanted to move to safer territory.

"The Godfather."

"Great," I said. Of course, people had claimed my grandfather was the basis for bits of Brando's performance. The jowly appearance. The Old World ways. The garden in back of the house.

In that moment, I wondered if God was trying to tell me something. Become a nun, Teddi. Do yourself a favor and become a nun.

"New topic."

He laughed good-naturedly. "You know…we've never discussed art. Who is your favorite painter?"

"I don't have one."

"Come on. None?"

"Robert, I know you may find this difficult to believe, but…the only time I have been in a museum was on school field trips."

"Really?"

"Please don't patronize me. You've seen my family's choice of decor. Granted, you've only been to one house, but suffice it to say, 'you've been to one, you've been to all.' Call it post-modern Mafia. We don't do art."

"Your mother collects Hummels. She mentioned it at dinner."

"Hummels? Little Swiss children with braids? Not art. No, what we need to discuss is your trip to the Giants game."

"I have the limo. I'm picking them all up at your parents' house—because that is where Sunday dinner is that particular Sunday. I have the limo bar stocked with Scotch, beer, red wine and vodka, according to the various favorites of your uncles and your father and your cousins. I think, my darling Teddi, that I am going to come sailing through the football game smelling like a rose."

I held up my hands. "Whoa there, cowboy. *Many* a man

has thought he could handle an event with the Marcellos and Gallos, but I assure you there is a plethora of unknowns you haven't even *begun* to think about."

"You underestimate me," he teased.

"For instance, strip club stop-off. Where do you stand?"

"Why would we stop at a strip club?"

"Why is the sky blue? Why is the grass green? Why does the pope wear a really big hat?"

"O-ka-a-a-ay." I could almost see him thinking, his brain whirring through the possibilities. "I say no because I am dating you and that would make them think I am not a good guy."

I shook my head. "You poor, poor fool."

"Damn. I say yes?"

"Of course you say yes. Men who say no are either gay or pussies. You don't want to be labeled either, trust me. But do you *enjoy* yourself at said strip club?"

"Jesus, Teddi, this is harder than taking the SATs and GREs combined. Enjoy myself at said strip club. I say yes, so they think I'm macho."

"Robert…" I chided playfully.

"God, my brain is going to explode. Help me out here, Teddi."

"No…you do *not* look like you are having *too* good of a time. Then they might think you are a little too devilish for the purer-than-the-driven-snow Teddi."

"Okay. Got it. Anything else?"

"We're just warming up."

"Test me again."

"You do not make any reference to the mob, the Mafia, the family business, anything that even hints at the fact that you think they are anything but a bunch of extremely well-compensated waste-management executives or concrete workers."

"Simple enough."

"But..."

He grinned and sighed, twirling pasta on his fork. "I knew there had to be one of those."

"You *do* need to be well versed in all the various mob movies. They love them."

"Not a problem. I love them, too."

"Would help if you knew a few of the best lines. The 'Fredo, you broke my heart' lines...you know, the best parts of the movies."

"Got it."

"Cigars."

"I take it I have to smoke them. That was obvious when I went to dinner."

I nodded.

"Should I be taking notes? Little crib sheets? Maybe I should write in a Sharpie up my arm."

I laughed out loud and stood and went over to his side of the table. He pushed his chair back, and I sat on his lap. "I think it's absolutely adorable that you're willing to put up with their idiosyncrasies."

"Is that what you call it? Well...I think you're absolutely adorable, and there's nothing I wouldn't do for you."

I leaned my head down and kissed him. He unbuttoned my blouse and slid his hand inside my bra.

"Mmm," I said, pulling back. "Let's finish dinner."

"And dessert," he said, squeezing me.

"Actually...I made crème brûlée."

"You *do* know the way to a man's heart is through his stomach, don't you?"

I kissed him again. "There are a few other ways, too."

I climbed off his lap and returned to my chair. We finished dinner and then dessert. I brought out two sambucas with three coffee beans floating in the snifters.

"What time is it?" he asked.

"Eight-fifteen," I said, looking at my watch.

"Jerry's on."

"Well, then, let's watch him."

I actually had never watched Jerry Turner's show, other than as a three-second sound bite as I flipped to another station. We turned on the television. Upcoming was a segment, pretaped, of Robert's jailhouse interview with a rabbi who allegedly hired a hitman to kill his wife because she was insured for two *million* dollars, and he was deep in debt.

"This is very odd."

"What is?" he asked.

"I'm sitting next to the 'live' Robert Wharton while the television Robert Wharton yaks at me from, as Lady Di puts it, 'the idiot box.'"

"Yeah. Kind of weird. I remember the first time I saw myself on TV. It's sort of like hearing your voice on a tape recorder or answering machine. 'I don't sound like that, do I?'"

After Robert's segment, we watched Jerry Turner rip apart the D.A. for losing a major case. Next up was a celebrity he destroyed for being anti-American.

"How does he get people to be a guest on his show? No one stands a chance."

"Ego," Robert said. "People think that *they* will be the one to put the legendary Jerry Turner in his place."

"Never works out that way, does it?"

"Nope. Yeah, he's confrontational, but he's also prepared. And very smart."

"Sort of like Howard Stern."

"What do you mean?"

"Well, he may be a lot of things, but stupid isn't one of them. If you listen to him, you realize he's very prepared."

"You listen to Howard Stern?"

"No. Ju-Ju-B does sometimes."

"Who's Ju-Ju-B?"

"One of my assistant chefs."

I snuggled against Robert, and we watched the end of the program. But with my crazy work schedule, coupled with the juggling of dating someone for the first time in a long while, and my sleepless nights due to the dilemma of one Agent Petrocelli, I soon passed out.

"Teddi…Teddi…" Robert shook me gently.

"Hmm?" I checked my mouth to make sure I hadn't been drooling. "I'm so sorry." I yawned and stretched. "I've been burning the candle at both ends. Are there more than two ends?"

"It's okay, sweetie. Do you know you're adorable when you're asleep?"

Yeah. Because I didn't drool tonight. "What time is it?"

"Eleven-thirty. I've got to run. I have an early call tomorrow."

"All right." I stood. Had it been a week or so ago, I would have been halfway certain we would have slept together tonight. I would have been one hundred percent certain if Mark Petrocelli hadn't kissed me in such a passionate way as to muddle my head. I just needed some distance from the whole incident. "Will you call me tomorrow?"

"Sure. I've got a meeting with a potential source on Friday. But I will also touch base with you before Sunday to make sure I have all my rules straight regarding any and every eventuality that could occur while taking a limo full of your relatives to a Giants game."

I walked him to the door and hugged him. His arms wrapped around me perfectly and my breasts pressed against his chest. We kissed good-night. After he left, I locked and bolted the door.

I turned to look at all the dishes. I had slept so heavily on the couch. But I was in no mood to start cleaning up. They could wait until morning. I walked back to my bedroom, slipped out of my clothes and into my bed. Exhaustion had finally caught up with me. I slept soundly until the morning.

chapter 19

Office Memorandum: United States Government
TO: David Cameron
FROM: Mark Petrocelli, Special Agent in
Charge, Federal Bureau of Investigation
SUBJECT: Wiretap report, Anthony (Tony)
Mancetti's apartment (Grandson of Angelo
Marcello)

11:45 p.m.

Diana Kent: Tony?
Tony Mancetti: What, baby?
Diana Kent: Two questions.
Tony Mancetti: Shoot.
Diana Kent: Shoot what?
Tony Mancetti: I mean go. Ask me.
Diana Kent: What did you think of Robert?

Tony Mancetti: He was okay. Not the kind of
guy I pictured Teddi with. All right…I don't
like him. And neither does Poppy.
Diana Kent: Yes. But would you expect her
to marry someone connected?
Tony Mancetti: (Laughing)
Diana Kent: What's so terribly funny?
Tony Mancetti: When you try to talk family shorthand. That's what's so funny. And
no. I'd break her legs if she ended up with
some soldier. She's too smart. Way too
smart. But I also didn't picture a stuffed
shirt, either.
Diana Kent: If I tell you something, will
you promise not to break anyone's legs?
Tony Mancetti: Tell me.
Diana Kent: Promise me first.
Tony Mancetti: Can't promise if you don't
tell me.
Diana Kent: Promise me.
Tony Mancetti: I can't resist you when you
pout like that. God, don't tell anyone I am
absolutely fuckin' whipped, Diana. All
right…I promise.
Diana Kent: All right, then. Tonight, when
I was alone with Robert in the living room,
Teddi was cooking…. Well…I think Robert
Wharton was coming on to me.
Tony Mancetti: That motherfucker—
Diana Kent: Now, don't be difficult. You
promised, after all. But I really think he
was making a play. Anyway, he is giving me

the creeps, and I don't think he's good for
Teddi. At all.

Tony Mancetti: I'll fuckin' kill him, Diana.
Coming on to my girlfriend *and* fuckin' pulling this bullshit on Teddi.

Diana Kent: Don't be so cross. I'm a big
girl, and I have handled lots of pompous
asses before. And maybe I was mistaken, but
I don't think so.

Tony Mancetti: You gonna tell her? 'Cause
that motherfucker hurts her, I'll kill him.

Diana Kent: Well, that brings me to question number two.

Tony Mancetti: What question?

Diana Kent: Remember? I asked you if I
could bring up two questions. So I asked
you about Robert, and now I have to ask
you something else.

Tony Mancetti: Shoot.

Diana Kent: I got it this time. Means "go."
What do you think your family would say if
Teddi ended up with…let's just say someone
from law enforcement?

Tony Mancetti: A cop? Jeez. She seein' a
cop, too?

Diana Kent: Not exactly. But what if I told
you that a PR agent spends her time with
people, people, people. Putting parties together, putting people together, hooking up
this magazine writer with that singer. Making connections. And I have gotten so good
at it that…well, let's just say that I have

an uncanny ability to spot when two people
are made for each other.

Tony Mancetti: And you're saying my cousin
Teddi should be with a cop?

Diana Kent: Sort of.

Tony Mancetti: Like a fix-up? You know
this cop?

Diana Kent: In a manner of speaking, yes.
We discussed Jimmy Choo shoes. But that's
neither here nor there. When the two of them
are near each other, you can just see the
sparks. So my question is, what would your
family say?

Tony Mancetti: I guess it would depend. I
mean, I've got two second cousins in the
NYPD. One of my father's cousins is a fire-
man. I would say that it would depend on
the cop. I mean, if he freaked out over us
betting on football and you know…things
like the truckload of shoes we got, then I
don't know. But if he was really the one
for Teddi, and he wasn't a fuckin' asshole,
then I guess it might be all right. Anything would be better than this Robert jerk.
Would help if the cop was Italian, ya know?

Diana Kent: How positively excellent.

Tony Mancetti: Come here. Take down your
hair.

Diana Kent: Mmm.

Tony Mancetti: I don't want to turn out the
light. I want to see you.

Diana Kent: I want to see you, too.

Tony Mancetti: You know you're my girl, right?

Diana Kent: Yes. And you're my guy.

Tony Mancetti: You won't go back to England, will you?

Diana Kent: Ever?

Tony Mancetti: Not like that…it's just—

Diana Kent: Shh. We'll figure it all out. Now, let me see you…

Tony Mancetti: God, you're fuckin' perfect. My thunderbolt.

chapter 20

I slept eight hours or more after my date with Robert, plus couch time. But when I didn't wake up rested, I decided it was time to go see my horse.

Poppy Marcello has always had many interests and many hobbies. He likes Cuban cigars, and he follows boxing. He enjoys playing bocce ball on sawdust in the back of his restaurant. He likes to sit around with his family every Sunday and eat until no one can move. He relaxes in his wood shop and his garden. And he likes horses. Racehorses.

Teddi Bear's Folly was a beautiful, sleek, black Thoroughbred. Poppy bought her six years ago. Poppy's trainer, Arturo "Doc" Decicco trained Teddi Bear's Folly along with a dozen other horses at a farm in the Catskills. Some of the horses did well. A couple were trotters—raced with the carts. The farm never lost money, but then again, it didn't make money. Because the horses were a passion, that was just fine. The best of Poppy's horses, Valentine Vegas All-the-

Way, was set out to stud and that brought in fees. And so, the farm was a beautiful place that did okay for the family, and when my cousins and I were younger, we would go there in the summers for a vacation, swim in the pond, fish and enjoy the fresh air that we lacked in Brooklyn and Queens.

Teddi Bear's Folly, though, was a money loser. In fact, she had never run a race. Not ever. Actually, she had *started* many a race, but she never finished. She would start out at the gate okay, but inevitably, on the last lap, she would stumble, or suddenly lose her stride. Doc thought perhaps she'd do better in shorter races. But that didn't work, either. So, instead, Teddi Bear's Folly was put out to pasture and became little more than an overgrown pet.

I begged Uncle Lou to let me borrow his Lincoln Town Car. Living in Manhattan, I didn't need a car of my own. Uncle Lou agreed, so he and Tony did their rounds of the pizza ventures in Tony's sports car and dropped off the Lincoln to me around 11:00 a.m. Driving a Town Car is kind of like driving a Sherman tank. The trunk was big enough to store several bodies in—a fact not lost on me. I always wondered what would happen if someone applied luminol to the trunk. But then, as I often did, I pushed the idea from my mind.

The car, a long black monstrosity, was housed in a parking garage. She was polished to a sheen, and though I rarely drove her, she was a smooth ride. I had learned to drive on my mother's maroon Cadillac. My father let me use his Town Car once I got my license. In short, I wasn't a woman who drove a compact car. I drove big cars—and loved them. And every once in a while, I liked to take a drive up the New York Thruway to the farm to visit my Folly.

The day was beyond brisk and had moved into frigid. I dressed for the weather, feeling like the Pillsbury Dough-boy in my parka and hat. I looked like a beefy guy. I had on blue jeans and my black riding boots. I had felt tense on the streets of Manhattan, but once I got into the mountains, I felt like I was in heaven. I rolled down the windows and blasted the heat, feeling the sting on my cheeks and gulping in the fresh air. Then I decided enough with the cold and rolled the windows back up and just enjoyed the scenery. Eventually, I arrived at the farm. Doc came out to welcome me in the gravel driveway.

"Teddi? Is that you? I barely recognize you in that big coat. You should have phoned. I would have set up the guest bedroom for you and had Frannie make you some lunch." He kissed each of my cheeks, pink from the cold, his handlebar mustache tickling me.

"No fuss. Not staying overnight. I just felt like taking Folly out."

"I'll saddle her up."

"Thanks, Doc."

He went off to the barn and I walked slowly behind him, feeling myself relax. When I got to the corral, the horses' mouths and nostrils were half-hidden by their breath, curling into fog in front of their heads. The grass beneath them was dusted with snow, and the horses gathered together for warmth, hanging around the bale of hay they were nibbling.

Doc brought Folly out. I pulled an apple from my coat pocket and offered it to her. She came and nuzzled me. I slipped my foot into the stirrups and waved to Doc.

"Be careful, Teddi. She bucks and you fall on the frozen ground and you'll break something for sure."

"I'll be careful. She's not skittish."

Skittish? Teddi's Folly was a step up from glue. Forget digging your heels in, or even a crop to get her to move. She *walked* everywhere, which was fine by me. As we walked out into the woods, I began to tell Folly my troubles. I imagined that she understood in some wise, equine way.

Did I really care about Robert, or was it that he was so different from my family that attracted me? And what was it about Agent Petrocelli that I found so damn appealing? I imagined Folly telling me it was his biceps. "No," I said. "It's more than that." He had perfected the smirk. But he also had this incredible way of seeing into me. Who could explain chemistry? And it was chemistry I feared from when I was a little girl.

And what was I to do with Quinn? With the cookbook? It didn't matter once I was on Folly's back. I rode and just let my troubles fade away. As I breathed out, the air turned to clouds of vapor, and I imagined it taking my confusion with it. Not that it helped me make up my mind about anything.

I stayed at the farm for supper and drove back to the city very late. I called Uncle Lou from my cell phone and told him I would put the car in my building's garage and he could get it the next day. Back in the city, I decided to drive by the restaurant to see if I could catch Quinn and have our sambuca together. We needed all the luck we could get. I also was praying Tatiana hadn't quit. She was our longest front-of-house employee, and she stayed for Quinn. Once the two of them actually got together, I assumed it would end in disaster like every other woman.

I pulled up to the curb. The lights were out, but very often Quinn would go into the small office to count the receipts. I took out my keys and got ready to open the door and deactivate the alarm.

Suddenly, out of nowhere, tires squealed on the quiet street and a black sedan pulled opposite the restaurant, its passenger-side window down and a gun firing out of it. I literally saw the car in a blur, and at the same time, it was truly as if my life flashed before my eyes, my whole world going by in slow motion. I saw my mother and father in my mind, my first pony ride, sitting with my grandmother and the photo of Mariella, my grandmother's funeral, my high school crush, meeting Diana, picking out the linen for Teddi's with Quinn, the first dollar Quinn and I ever made, framed on the wall of Teddi's behind the bar—and the first time I laid eyes on Mark Petrocelli. All this, I swear, in the time it took me to blink my eyes.

A bullet shattered the front window of Teddi's, and a spray of bullets hit the windshield of Uncle Lou's car. No one was on the street, and for the life of me, I don't know why, but I froze. I didn't duck, I didn't fall to the sidewalk. My breath left me, and I couldn't even muster up a scream. This wasn't happening, I told myself. This wasn't happening.

From the opposite direction, a blue van sped and blocked the remaining path of the gunshots. I saw Mark Petrocelli and another agent fly out the back doors, and Mark reached me and pulled me to the ground so fast and hard a pain shot through my shoulder as we hit the sidewalk, his biceps curling around my head to protect me.

Within minutes, cop cars surrounded the black sedan, whose tires the FBI had shot. The car was driven by none other than Crazy Chris Corelli, I could see, though Mark and I were still lying on the sidewalk. I don't know who was breathing harder—him or me. My teeth chattered from shock more than cold, and I finally looked up at him.

"That transfer to white-collar crime can't come fast enough," he whispered, his face pale.

"Amen," I whispered, and buried my head into his chest. "Is Quinn okay?"

"He went home a half hour ago. We saw Corelli and decided to stay."

Slowly, hearing cops' voices all around and shouting on the street, we stood. My hands shook as I opened Teddi's, desperately wanting a drink. Mark and his partner came in. I paged Quinn, who soon arrived and took me into his arms, kissing the top of my head and then pulling back every few seconds or so to make sure I was "really in one piece." I was still wearing my stupid bulky ski jacket, and I let Quinn take it off of me.

"You swear you're not hurt?" he said.

I nodded. "Just my shoulder, from where I landed on the sidewalk."

Quinn leaned in very close to me and whispered in my ear so quiet, no one else could hear. "Corelli is a dead man."

Quinn called my father, Uncle Lou and Tony, and they came, along with my Poppy, who, from his wild hair and striped pajama top with dress trousers, was obviously roused from bed.

Mark said to them, "The car, the bulky jacket. They thought she was Lou. Had to be. Even Corelli looked unnerved he almost killed her."

"Teddi Bear." Poppy held me to him, tears streaming down his face. My father had four double Scotches in rapid succession, and Uncle Lou and Tony were answering questions from the police.

Within twenty minutes, the family attorney, George Gri-selli, arrived and called this "random street violence." He had an in at one of the newspapers. He'd try to influence how it played out, I knew.

Mark looked helplessly at me. In a room full of people, he had to act as if he didn't know me as more than his assignment. And I knew I had never so desperately wanted to be held by a man in my life.

Within three hours, we had locked up again, called Quinn's cousin Andrew, who owned a glass company, and swept the sidewalk of glass. I had waved solemnly at Mark, whom my father must have shaken hands with forty times to thank him for saving my life, and was ushered home by my dad and Uncle Lou, while Tony took Poppy back to his house. In my apartment, my father called my mother and told her everything was going to be okay.

Diana came stumbling out of her bedroom in a green silk bathrobe.

"What's going on?"

"Teddi was almost shot at the restaurant," Uncle Lou said.

"What?" Diana was to me in two seconds flat, sitting next to me on the couch and stroking my hair. I wanted to cry, but I was too numb.

I nodded. "I had borrowed Uncle Lou's car. They thought I was him."

"Oh, good Lord, that's insane. He has a bald spot."

Uncle Lou patted the back of his head.

"I was wearing a hat, Di. They couldn't tell. A hat and a big ski jacket. I did kind of look like a guy."

"Well, what happened? Did they get this guy?"

My father, whose face was still pale, his pompadour flat and pieces of hair askew and falling on his forehead, said,

"An FBI agent saved her, of all fuckin' things. This family owes that man a debt of gratitude. An Italian, no less. We'll send him a case of wine. Something. If anything had happened to her…" His voice trailed off and he walked away and into the kitchen.

I looked at my watch. It was near dawn. "Guys…I'm about to keel over. Why don't you go home? I want to go to bed."

"Of course," Uncle Lou said. "But I'll be right out on the sidewalk in front of this apartment building. You girls are safe."

They left after kissing me, and Di started to cry.

"Di…I'm okay."

"This is the scariest thing that's ever happened. What if you had been shot? It was James Bond who saved you, wasn't it?"

I nodded.

"Oh, Teddi, doesn't that show you something?"

"It shows me he's still staking out my restaurant."

"You can't mean that."

I shook my head. "I know. I don't."

"What's going to happen to the men who tried to shoot you?"

"It's a rival family. There'll be a sit-down with the head of that family…after the guy finishes his prison sentence. They caught him red-handed so there'll be some kind of retribution."

"He deserves it, the bastard. Our Teddi. Our dear, darling Teddi. Do you want me to make you some breakfast?"

I stared at her. "Di, you don't even do toast right."

"How about a spot of tea and then off to bed?"

"Just bed will be fine."

She tried to help me up from the couch.

"Di—" I held up my hands. "I can still walk like a normal person."

"Right-o. It's just so scary."

I hugged her. "I'm okay."

"And Tony? Where's he in all this?"

"He drove my grandfather home. He'll be here stalking us more than ever, I'm sure."

We got to my bedroom and I hugged her again, then I went in, shut the door, stripped down to my underwear and went to sleep.

When I woke up, it was one o'clock in the afternoon, and I almost felt as if I had dreamt the entire thing, right down to that "life flashing in front of my eyes" thing. It was as if it had never happened.

But of course, it had.

Later that night, I showed up at work, much to the astonishment of Quinn.

"You were practically assassinated and you're at work?"

"Assassinated?" I hissed at him. "I'm not one of the Kennedys, Quinn."

"Call it what you want. I'm freaked out. And so is the family—both sides. Take a look in the dining room."

I spun my head around and was instantly filled with love—and laughter. Every table was full—of family. They'd taken over the place, including my Poppy.

"Hello, everyone," I said as I stepped into the main room.

Everyone gave a little wave. My mother stood up and came over and hugged me to her. "I promised myself I wouldn't cry."

"Ma…"

"I know. I'm just terrified."

I brushed a tear away and said to my family, "I better get back in the kitchen."

There, in the kitchen, Ju-Ju-B and Leon were arguing over the radio station.

"Hey, boss lady," Leon said. "We didn't expect you."

I shrugged. "Get shot at, go to work, it's all in a day."

Ju-Ju-B came over to me with a meat cleaver. "Anyone touches a hair on your head, Teddi and—" He pretended to draw the cleaver across his throat.

"Meat cleaver vs. Uzi. Fair fight." I grinned at him. "Now, back to work. We got a packed house."

"What's this 'head' your family is all requesting?" Leon looked at the ticket in front of him.

"We don't carry it," I said. "Fix them all the antipasto platters."

We worked hard to feed them all, then Quinn said he'd close up alone. Tony drove me back to my apartment. He went into Di's bedroom, and I tried to relax. I sat at the small desk in my room and composed recipes and stories. I remembered stories of hard times when the family first came to America, and stories of fabled gangsters who liked certain veal dishes. I was having fun when the phone rang. I assumed it was Quinn asking me something.

"Yeah?"

"Teddi? It's Robert."

"Oh, hi, Robert."

"I just heard about the shooting. They're trying to play it off like it was random violence or some giant coincidence, but come on. It was a hit. I'm surprised you weren't swarmed by the media."

"The Mafia isn't the news it once was." I eyed my answering machine, showing I had twenty-one messages. I guessed some of them were media. I groaned.

"What?"

"Nothing."

"Are you all right?"

"Yeah. I am."

"Can I come see you?"

"Not tonight, Robert. I am just laying low. It's been an insane twenty-four hours."

"All right. Promise me you'll be careful."

"Of course I will."

"All right. Good night."

"Good night, Robert."

I waited, as I wrote stories down, to hear from Mark. But he never called. I told myself he was busy with cases. He was busy investigating the Corellis. He was busy arranging his transfer, but in my heart, I didn't believe that. Maybe, after nearly seeing me shot, he realized our worlds were too far apart.

I sighed. It was time to stop mooning over him. Time to grow up and face a hefty dose of reality. He wasn't my thunderbolt. He couldn't be. If he was, we'd be together. Or perhaps, like Mariella and Mario, we'd just been driven apart by circumstances beyond our control.

Suddenly, I felt a surge to write the story of Mariella and Uncle Mario and include a recipe. I picked up the picture frame from among all the little silver frames of family. Mariella was wearing a suit and white gloves. Her long black hair blew around her face, and she was laughing. I would name their recipe Mariella's Broken Heart Soup. It was a lemon-based soup my grandmother said Uncle Mario made when she went to visit them. The whole apartment smelled like lemon. It was Mariella's favorite. Sour, not sweet.

★ ★ ★

"Hello?" Two days later, I held the phone against my still-sore shoulder as I chopped fresh basil in the kitchen of Teddi's.

"Hello, famous flatmate."

"Hello, Di."

"Anna just rang me. You already have two publishing houses bidding over you, and you haven't pulled together all the proposal yet."

"Really?"

"Yes, really. Teddi's will be very famous, and so will you."

"Well, luckily it's Quinn there in the front of the house sucking up to it all. And, naughty girl, you never came home last night."

"Oh, you have no idea."

"Really?"

"From a realm of sexual pleasure others only dream of."

"Really?" I asked, bemused.

"If George Michael was straight, and if he fucked me for hours with Wham! playing in the background, it could *not* do justice to what last night was. Unbelievable. I think your cousin has been struck mute."

"Poor Tony. Doesn't know what hit him."

"Poor Tony indeed." She laughed into the phone. "And you know…you never did rank the kiss from James Bond."

"I told you—it can't ever be."

"Nonetheless. Ranking?" Di always ranked everything.

"First."

"First?"

"Unfortunately, yes, because he'll never call me again. I need to concentrate on the cookbook. On Teddi's. Put it from my mind."

"We'll see."

"What's in that devious head of yours?"

"Nothing!" she sang into the phone brightly. "Must run."

I hung up the phone and went up front to tell Quinn the good news about the cookbook.

"I'm telling you, Teddi," Quinn said, "…we're going to be on the map!"

"Quinn, you are irrepressible, you know that?"

"And you are always too practical. So between the dreamer and the pragmatist lies the perfect combination."

"Maybe."

"Hey, Teddi…can I ask you something?"

"Sure."

"I didn't say anything that night, but whatever happened between you and the FBI guy?"

"Nothing."

"That's not the way it looked to me."

"What do you mean?"

"Come here." He took me by the hand and led me over to the wall. "You…looked like her—" he pointed to the copy of the picture of Mariella, the one from my room "—the night he came in here. The night you two had dinner together. Sometimes, Teddi, you should tell that 'practical' head of yours to shut up."

I turned to face Quinn. "He hasn't called since the night of the shooting. Whatever you saw that night, Quinn, the Marcello and Gallo baggage I drag around with me is just too much for Agent Petrocelli."

"Nah. Not that guy."

"Yes, that guy. And you know who *has* called me?"

"TV repairman."

"Yes."

"Come on, let's have a sambuca and talk about it."

"There's nothing to talk about, Quinn. Nothing at all." I turned on my heel and went back to the kitchen—my territory. Luis looked at me with his one eye. "And what do you want?" I snapped.

"Nothing, Teddi. I know better than to fuck with an Italian when she's angry. That's how I lost my eye."

"Oh," I said meekly, and tried to chop my basil a little less angrily. "Sorry."

"That's okay. This place is crazy. Crazy," he muttered.

"Luis," I said softly. "I kind of have to agree with you there."

chapter 21

Office Memorandum: United States Government
TO: David Cameron
FROM: Mark Petrocelli, Special Agent in Charge, Federal Bureau of Investigation
SUBJECT: Wiretap report, Anthony (Tony) Mancetti's phone line

7:30 p.m.

Tony Mancetti: Diana?
Diana Kent: Yes, lovie?
Tony Mancetti: I got some not-so-good news. About Teddi.
Diana Kent: What? What? Tell me before I have a heart attack. Is she hurt? Does it have to do with those Corelli people?

Tony Mancetti: No. This has to do with a broken heart.

Diana Kent: What?

Tony Mancetti: You know, we're not the kind of family that lets just anyone date our Teddi.

Diana Kent: Really? How shocking.

Tony Mancetti: Well...we did some checking.

Diana Kent: Who's "we"?

Tony Mancetti: Now, don't get mad.

Diana Kent: I won't get mad.

Tony Mancetti: My father made some—let's call them inquiries. Everyone was really upset after the shooting and everything. You know, being extra careful.

Diana Kent: And?

Tony Mancetti: That scumbag is using Teddi. He is planning on doing a show about the Marcello family. A huge two-hour special, and he was using her to get some access to us. Not only that—

Diana Kent: Robert? That bastard.

Tony Mancetti: I'm not done yet.

Diana Kent: There's more?

Tony Mancetti: A lot more.

Diana Kent: Oh, God! I can't stand it.

Tony Mancetti: He's bangin' some blonde. She does the show before Turner's.

Diana Kent: Nancy Austin?

Tony Mancetti: Bingo, baby! That's the one!

Diana Kent: I'll kill him myself. Serve him his shriveled testicles for breakfast.

Tony Mancetti: No. We have better plans.

Diana Kent: Tony—

Tony Mancetti: Nothing illegal. At least not very.

Diana Kent: What, then?

Tony Mancetti: You just leave it to the family. In the meantime, when all is said and done, you help Teddi get over her broken heart.

Diana Kent: I know just the cure for that. But you won't…kill Robert or anything?

Tony Mancetti: Never say things like that on the telephone, Diana. No. But we'll teach him a Marcello family lesson he won't soon forget.

chapter 22

Diana came in for dinner every night through Saturday. Tony, too. Besides everyone being over-the-top concerned for me, the two of them seemed determined to spur me on to make the book the greatest Italian-American cookbook ever published. Anna Friedman, with the taming of Quinn, was actually effusive on the phone as she pulled the proposal together and continued to pitch the idea to her favorite editors. Teddi's was busy, too. With Thanksgiving and Christmas literally around the corner, visitors flocked to Manhattan. Though we were crammed with regulars, out-of-towners laden with shopping bags seemed to find their way to our tables, too. Not to mention extra doses of Marcellos and Gallos. Pip would be pleased.

Quinn also seemed to settle down. Tatiana was glowing, and I guessed that could only mean he was with her for more than his usual one night. Chef Jeff's dreads were coming in. Life was making sense.

Sort of.

Robert called me daily, genuinely excited for the upcoming football game. And twice I spotted Mark Petrocelli, once outside my apartment building, once in the deli Diana and I frequented. Each time he avoided making eye contact with me, and I tried to pretend he wasn't there. He was a figment of my imagination. Robert was flesh and blood.

Sunday dinner was missing the contingent of men, except for some of my cousins—after all, Robert couldn't take them all.

My mother was in a foul mood. "You need an Italian, Teddi."

"*Now* she's fussy," I retorted. "*Now* she's fussy. Any man in Manhattan with a pulse has been fine for all these years, but now that I have someone, you can't stand to see me happy, can you?"

Her eyes welled.

"I'm sorry, Ma."

"I'm gonna cry again."

"Ma, I'm safe. Chris Corelli is on Riker's Island."

"Yeah, yeah. You're still off in Manhattan instead of here, where you belong."

Putting aside our differences, we compared recipes. Seems not *one* of my aunts or my mother used the same ricotta-and-sauce proportion for making eggplant parmigiana. Italian cooking, cooking in general, was about improvisation. About taste.

"It's like lovemaking," Aunt Rose offered.

"Lovemaking!" my mother scoffed.

"It is. A little give, a little take, a little of this, a little of that, and then…magic."

Di piped up, "A little magic. That's what we all need."

★ ★ ★

The Giants lost. A colossal loss that would surely have my uncles and father in a foul mood. This could only mean a visit to a strip club afterward to drown their sorrows in "tits and tonic," as my mother calls it. I hoped Robert remembered my coaching.

Di came into my room, and we watched *Law & Order* reruns. Di was very bad about remembering past episodes, so even if she saw one before, she was always surprised at the verdict.

Sometime around midnight, we both must have fallen asleep in my bed. Around two o'clock in the morning, the phone rang. I bolted awake.

Di grabbed it first, fumbling in the half light of the television.

"Hullo?…what?…what?!… *What!*"

I slapped her. "What's going on?"

"Oh, that's rich!

"Right-o!

"And his name is?

"Right-o!"

I slapped her again and she slapped me back.

She motioned for a pen and then wrote down an address.

Of a police station.

In Jersey.

"Well…" Diana said when she hung up the phone. "That was Tony."

"What?" I said, dread building in my gut.

"I'm afraid I've kept a secret from you. I took a vow of silence thingie. With Tony."

"Oh, God. Am I ready to hear this?"

"Well, perhaps we should get a drink. Not champagne. A stiff one."

She went to the living room, where we kept liquor in a cabinet, and returned with a bottle of vodka and two glasses. She poured us each a shot.

"I need this." She tossed hers back.

"What is it, Di?"

"Okay, then…your Robert…was cheating on you. With Nancy Austin. That stupid bottled blonde on before Turner."

I tossed back my vodka. "Oh, God. How do you know?"

"Well, there's more. He was ready to do a show on the Marcellos, lovebug. And he was using you to get to them, I'm afraid."

I suddenly lunged from the bed to the bathroom and hurled up the vodka. "Oh, my God! Oh, my God! What an idiot I am!" I slumped to the bathroom tile.

She came to the bathroom and bent over and stroked my hair. "Don't feel badly. Sometimes I throw up shots, too."

"Not that, Di…Robert. How could I have been so un-believably fucking stupid?"

Then she whispered, "More bad news…strike three…he came on to me. That night he was here for supper. My dear, dear Teddi, he's just an all-around lugubrious creep. I'm so very, very, sorry, pumpkin."

I looked up at her. "Did everyone know but me?"

"No. Most of this is a very recent turn of events."

"Does Quinn know?"

She nodded. "Tony told him."

"It must be serious. Quinn didn't even tease me tonight." I felt tears on my face. I had been trying to talk myself into liking Robert, when he hadn't deserved liking. I felt great racking sobs coming up from my gut where the vodka had been.

Di, like the wonderful best friend she has always been,

just let me bawl. She rubbed my back and occasionally passed me reams of Charmin to blow my nose.

Suddenly, I pulled myself up from the floor. "Oh, my God...Jersey police. What has my family done to him? I hate him, I hate him, but please tell me he is not in little pieces in the Meadowlands. Or fed into a meat grinder. He's not worth it. He's so not worth it."

"Uh, no. That was Tony. His one phone call. The family attorney—"

"Griselli?"

"Yes. He certainly does earn his keep, doesn't he? He is bailing out all of your relatives for public drunkenness and hijacking a limousine. Tony says that may be dismissed."

"And Robert?"

"Appears they let him think they were going to cut him into little pieces like you said, to rest with Jimmy Hoffman."

"Hoffa."

"Yes, him."

"And?"

"And they left him naked, in the frigid Jersey cold, locked out of his limo. He has frostbite on his pinky toe and is swearing he is suing. The toe may even fall off."

I looked at her, and despite my tears, we both started laughing. We laughed until we couldn't stand anymore, then we slumped down on the floor of my bedroom, in the doorway to the bathroom.

Di looked at me. "You are so neat. Your bathroom floor is so clean you can eat off of it. Mine is a mess."

"Yes, I know."

"But you are a mess. You are not a pretty crier, Teddi."

"Is anyone?"

"Well, ever notice in Hollywood movies when the actresses cry, snot never dribbles down, their noses don't get red. They don't get splotchy."

"Yes. But that's not real life."

The phone rang.

"One of my uncles, no doubt. I should hate them, but for once, I think they're all wonderful. I can't wait to kiss them all. I hope Robert froze his testicles off." I lifted the phone.

"Teddi?"

"Yes?"

"Mark."

"Oh, my God."

"I know I should have called. I just had to do some thinking."

"One minute." I covered the phone. "It's James Bond," I whispered to Di.

"I believe this is my exit. Go get him, Octopussy."

She left my bedroom, shutting the door behind her. But not without kissing the top of my head first. Boy, she was becoming a real Mafia girlfriend—her first arrest of her boyfriend since they're together and she was almost happy about it.

"Hello, Mark."

"Seen the news? Your entire family's in lockup."

"Hadn't realized that would make the news."

"Sort of a light piece."

"They telephoned from the precinct."

"Robert Wharton deserved it. Nothing will stick. Wanted you to know that. Nothing. I'll make sure of that."

"Thank you."

"I'm really sorry about that Wharton, Teddi."

"It's all right," I sniffled at sympathy from Mark. I exhaled, regaining my composure. "I have to be honest. He wasn't rocking my world, much as I was trying to talk myself into it."

"You remember what we called it?"

"What?"

"You weren't struck by the thunderbolt."

"Oh, that. No…I guess I wasn't…. So, Mark, sell any shoes today?"

"Today was a good day. Sold a few pairs. Made a few people happy. Also heard about one woman…got her toes pinched a bit. Felt badly about that."

"She'll recover."

"I'm not going to stay away from you, you know."

"What?"

"Can't. Holding you on that sidewalk while bullets flew overhead? I never want to go through that again. I told myself I couldn't take it. Pops Petrocelli once told me, 'Mark, you only get hit by the thunderbolt once.' You're it. My thunderbolt. I'll get my reassignment. Soon."

"You'd do that?"

"I'd do that."

"I'm so sorry."

"I'm not. I've been waiting for my thunderbolt my whole life."

"So what are you wearing, Agent Petrocelli?"

"I'm calling you from home. From bed. Nothing but my boxers."

I smiled, thinking of him, perfect FBI haircut and all, lying in his bed in boxer shorts talking to me with that smirky, sly grin on his face that he always seemed to have around me.

"I'm a boxer gal myself."

"And what are you wearing?"

"My clothes. Di and I fell asleep on my bed until we were rudely awakened by a jailhouse telephone call at two. Jailhouse calls are kind of common in my family."

"Really? I thought your parents were schoolteachers."

"Protesters. Always arrested. You know. No nukes…." I stood and, balancing the phone, started taking off my clothes.

"What are you doing? I can hear you moving around."

"Getting naked. What else would I be doing when talking to my thunderbolt?"

"You know that kiss?"

"Which one?"

"Not the end-of-your-nose Central Park one. The kiss. *The* kiss."

"Yeah."

"Pretty intense."

"Yes. Pretty intense. Better than Bruce Springsteen."

"You've kissed Bruce Springsteen?"

"No. It's a silly game Di plays. She rates the kisses in her life with George Michael—of his Wham! days, not his Satanic-look goatee days—being the pinnacle."

"Has she kissed George Michael?"

"No."

"Isn't he gay?"

"Yes, but it's just imagination so sexuality doesn't count. And Tony is her first kiss. First place. And you have displaced my mystical Springsteen kiss."

"Springsteen, huh? I can handle that."

"Can you, now?"

"Are you naked now?"

"Yes."

He moaned. "You drive me wild, Teddi. When you came

out of the kitchen all hot and tired, I knew it. I mean…you were so real. So absolutely real."

"So can a woman with Mafia chic and an FBI agent find true happiness?"

"Can I come over and try to show you they can?"

"I'll be waiting."

It was almost dawn before he got to my apartment. The city was starting to rise. Diana was blow-drying and singing to Wham! And there was a knock on the door.

I opened it. He came in the door and kissed me, as strongly and passionately as the night at the restaurant. We kissed and made our way to the couch.

Diana came out to see us, dressed for work.

"I couldn't have created a happier ending if I had engineered it all myself. If it isn't James Bond and Octopussy. How are you?"

"Diana…" He smiled.

"Just because you're making nice with my flatmate now doesn't mean I've forgotten about my pair of shoes, you know. One pair of Jimmy Choos. Jimmy bloody Choos!"

"And what about all the pairs you got from Vito?"

"Oh, God." Her face went pale. "Are you going to handcuff me? I'll return them."

"Relax, Diana…. It seems the Marcellos are honest waste management executives. You can keep the shoes."

"Good. We'll call it even, then."

I snuggled against Mark, aware of how delicious he smelled.

"You two make a cute couple."

"Don't know if my boss will think so, but…"

"Your boss?" I turned to him. "Wait until my family finds out."

Diana just smiled. "I think they'll think it's grand. Simply grand! And like I said...just *think* of the meet-cute story you can tell your grandkids!"

chapter 23

One Year Later

BOOKSIGNING
Meet Teddi Marcello Gallo
Author: *Italian Style: Cooking with the Marcellos*

There it was.

I was an author.

People crowded the Barnes & Noble near Teddi's ever since I did a morning television show with my Poppy Marcello and we cooked rigatoni. He can charm the pants off a jury...he can charm the pants off the viewers of morning television.

A lot has happened in a year.

First of all, I've had to get used to signing my name. A lot. People bring the book into the restaurant. And then the signings. Quinn was always the "front of the house" guy, but I've adjusted.

What else?

Chef Jeff and Leon have dreads now. Long dreads with multicolored rubber bands.

Ju-Ju-B told us his real name is Horace. We still call him Ju-Ju-B. And honestly, after all this time it suits him. And we don't know why.

Lady Di and Tony are engaged. He bought her a two-and-a-half-carat rock. From some guy. So it doesn't have a receipt and a pale blue Tiffany box. It's still gorgeous. Uncle Lou has set Tony up in a bakery. He is out of the "other" family business for good, except for when anyone comes across Jimmy Choos that have "fallen from a truck," or Gucci bags, or any one of the dozens of things Diana is thrilled to have fall from the sky. In fact, she *loves* things that fall from trucks and is a walking British-talking Mafia princess.

If you had told me two years ago that I would end up being related by marriage to Diana Kent, I would have said you were crazy. But strange as it seems, the two of them fit together. Tony is rough around the edges, and she is all British polish and wit, and yet...when they are in a room, there is no doubt that what they have is real. He's learned to like Broadway and to swill martinis with the PR A-list crowd. And her father likes him. Or likes seeing Diana so over the moon. And Diana gets a family full of Marcellos...no more smiling and nodding for her! She gets overbearing, argumentative, dysfunctional, with some food issues thrown in. And she couldn't be happier.

Teddi's is packed every night of the week. We're opening a second location, have repaid our loans entirely, and Pip no longer has a case of hemorrhoids about us. We're thriving, and a recent review gave us three stars. No, it's not four, but I was happy.

Chris Corelli got five years for the attempt on my life, and another ten years for his illegal guns, including the two guns in his trunk, plus some more time thrown in for the heroin he had in his car. My Poppy sat down with Don Corelli, and he promised him no retribution if the Corellis backed off, which they did. And then Poppy surprised everyone by retiring and naming Uncle Lou as the new don. But even Uncle Lou seems to want to take it easy. He wants to live to see grandbabies. So maybe the last of the last of the Mafia are dying down.

Poppy, though retired, is still as wily as ever. He still pulls hundreds out from behind my ear and seems to think I am twelve.

Quinn…ah, Quinn. Well, he and Tatiana are expecting a baby—a girl. And no, that doesn't mean he's settled down. He's as incorrigible as ever—just ask my agent, Anna Friedman, who moons over him like she was twelve. But…he stays faithful, if flirtatious. And Tatiana's gorgeous enough to handle it. They got a place together near our new location, and after the baby is born and Tatiana can again fit in a size-two dress, they plan on making it legal down at City Hall.

My mother still calls me daily to remind me that my biological clock is ticking.

My brother Michael's television show was canceled, but he landed a small role in a new superhero movie and is on location in Romania. He says it's cold there.

Robert Wharton was fired for ethical reasons. Even journalists have some sort of standards. Last I heard he had hightailed it back to Philadelphia.

The blonde he was fucking moved on to bigger fish. She's with Jerry Turner now.

And after Robert Wharton lost his pinkie toe in what is now simply known as the "frostbite incident" in the family, Jerry Turner decided he wasn't so interested in doing an exposé on the Marcellos after all.

And I suppose that leaves me and Mark.

Well, let's just say Poppy gave him the okay after a lengthy sit-down during which, Mark—thank God for his Italian heritage—actually ate some lamb head. He was reassigned to some sort of banking scam, and he's thinking about leaving the bureau to start his own private investigation firm.

My father loves Mark because Mark saved my life.

And I love him, too. When Diana and Tony get married, we plan on getting engaged—I don't want to steal any of her limelight. And then he'll move into my apartment.

He is my thunderbolt. From that first night he stepped out of that van. I was just too afraid to see it.

And at night…he comes to me and we play with his handcuffs.

The Marcello Family Gravy

1 can (28 oz) imported* Italian tomatoes
1 small can (8 oz) tomato sauce
¼ cup extra virgin olive oil
4 or 5 crushed fresh garlic cloves
1½ T tomato paste
½ small onion chopped
1 T (about - to taste) chicken granules or bouillon paste
big grind or two of fresh pepper
(no salt)
handful of chopped/shredded fresh basil
2 T unsalted butter
¼ cup fresh parsley
*Put tomatoes through food mill—I use imported San Marzano (if I can find) tomatoes. Any imported Italian tomatoes will do.

Heat EVO oil in saute pan add onion and cook for a minute or so, add garlic. Do not brown. Add rest of ingredients. Simmer for about 10 minutes. Add my secret incredient (2T of unsalted butter). Add chopped fresh parsley, about 1/4 cup. Either serve over pasta or cool and refrigerate.
For a change can add some chopped black olives or lightly sauteed mushrooms.

Mangia!
Enjoy…with someone you love.

On sale now

girls' night in

21 of today's hottest female authors

1 fabulous short-story collection

And all for a good cause.

Featuring *New York Times* bestselling authors

Jennifer Weiner (author of *Good in Bed*),
Sophie Kinsella (author of *Confessions of a Shopaholic*),
Meg Cabot (author of *The Princess Diaries*)

Net proceeds to benefit War Child, a network of organizations dedicated to helping children affected by war.

Also featuring bestselling authors...

Carole Matthews, Sarah Mlynowski, Isabel Wolff, Lynda Curnyn, Chris Manby, Alisa Valdes-Rodriguez, Jill A. Davis, Megan McCafferty, Emily Barr, Jessica Adams, Lisa Jewell, Lauren Henderson, Stella Duffy, Jenny Colgan, Anna Maxted, Adèle Lang, Marian Keyes and Louise Bagshawe

RED DRESS INK™   WAR child®

www.RedDressInk.com   www.WarChildusa.org

Available wherever trade paperbacks are sold.

™ is a trademark of the publisher.
The War Child logo is the registered trademark of War Child.

RDIGNITRR

Another fabulous read by Erica Orloff

Diary of a Blues Goddess

Georgia Ray Miller dreams of abandoning her life
as a cheesy wedding singer and becoming a
"blues goddess," but her doubts keep getting in
the way. Besides, living in a haunted (former)
brothel with her hippie grandma, surrogate
boyfriend and an infamous drag queen is enough
to distract her from making a change.

It is not until she comes across a diary left
behind by her long-lost aunt that Georgia
starts to sing a different tune.

**Here's how: Try RED DRESS INK books
on for size & receive two FREE gifts!**

Bombshell
by Lynda Curnyn

As Seen on TV
by Sarah Mlynowski

YES! Send my two FREE books.
There's no risk and no purchase required—ever!

Please send me my two FREE books and bill me just 99¢ for shipping and handling. I may keep the books and return the shipping statement marked "cancel." If I do not cancel, about a month later I will receive 2 additional books at the low price of just $11.00 each in the U.S. or $13.56 each in Canada, a savings of over 15% off the cover price (plus 50¢ shipping and handling per book*). I understand that accepting the two free books places me under no obligation ever to buy any books. I can always return a shipment and cancel at any time. Even if I never buy another book from Red Dress Ink, the free books are mine to keep forever.

160 HDN D34M   360 HDN D34N

Name (PLEASE PRINT)

Address   Apt. #

City   State/Prov.   Zip/Postal Code

*Want to try another series? Call 1-800-873-8635
or order online at www.TryRDI.com/free.*

In the U.S. mail to: 3010 Walden Ave., P.O. Box 1867, Buffalo, NY 14240-1867
In Canada mail to: P.O. Box 609, Fort Erie, ON L2A 5X3

*Terms and prices subject to change without notice. Sales tax applicable in N.Y.
**Canadian residents will be charged applicable provincial taxes and GST.

All orders subject to approval. Offer limited to one per household.
® and ™ are trademarks owned and used by the trademark owner and/or its licensee.

© 2004 Harlequin Enterprises Ltd.

**RED
DRESS
INK**

RDI04-TR